BRETT BEAN

ZOO
PATROL
SQUAD

A NEW SHERIFF
IN TOWN

PENGUIN WORKSHOP

NOTE FROM THE AUTHOR

This book was made entirely during the COVID-19 pandemic. I laughed,
I cried, and I escaped in creating this book. I hope it does the same for you.
It's dedicated to all of us. Our lives are a story, so make it a good one.

ABOUT THE CREATOR

Brett Bean is an author, illustrator, and designer whose work has
been featured across film, TV, comics, children's books, and more. He has lots of
artwork and designs on his website, brettbean.com. He works from Los Angeles.

To learn more about the Zoo Patrol Squad, go to zoopatrolsquad.com.

W

PENGUIN WORKSHOP
An imprint of Penguin Random House LLC, New York

First published in the United States of America by Penguin Workshop,
an imprint of Penguin Random House LLC, New York, 2021

Copyright © 2021 by Brett Bean

PENGUIN is a registered trademark and PENGUIN WORKSHOP is a trademark of
Penguin Books Ltd, and the W colophon is a registered trademark of Penguin Random House LLC.

Visit us online at penguinrandomhouse.com.

Library of Congress Control Number: 2021012722

Manufactured in China

ISBN 9780593226605   10 9 8 7 6 5 4 3 2 1 HH

The publisher does not have any control over and does not assume any responsibility
for author or third-party websites or their content.

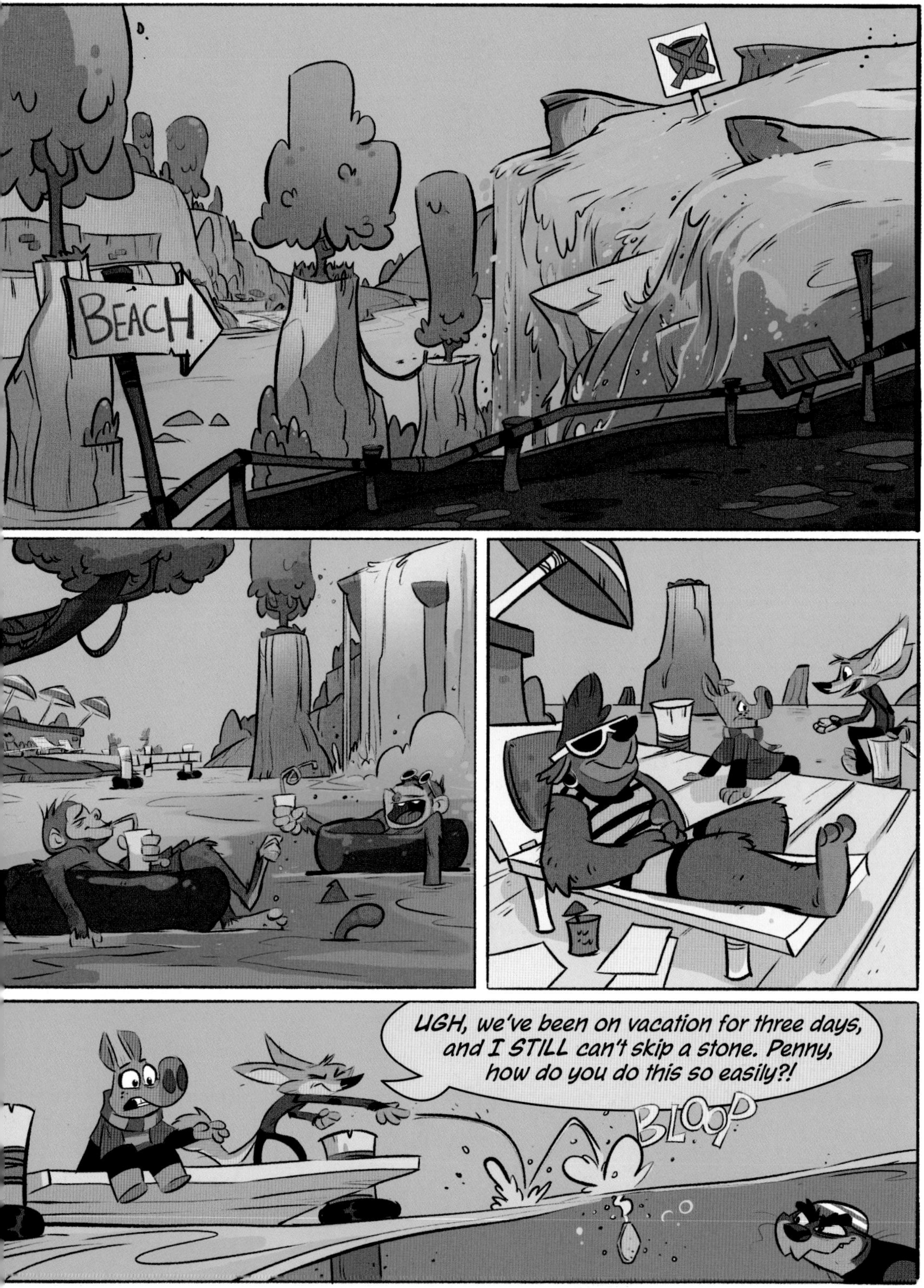
BEACH
UGH, we've been on vacation for three days, and I STILL can't skip a stone. Penny, how do you do this so easily?!
BLOOP

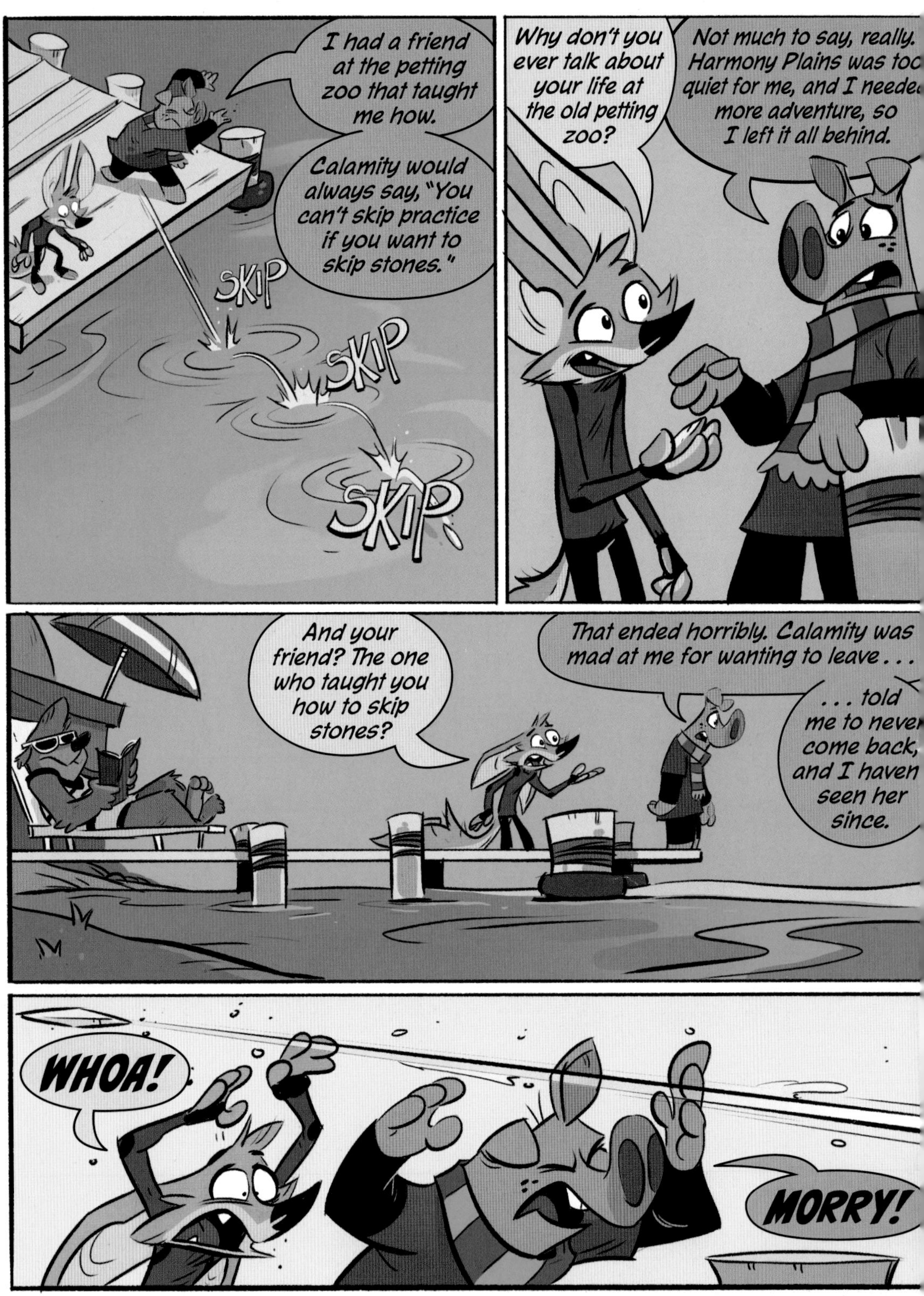
I had a friend at the petting zoo that taught me how.
Calamity would always say, "You can't skip practice if you want to skip stones."
SKIP
SKIP
SKIP
Why don't you ever talk about your life at the old petting zoo?
Not much to say, really. Harmony Plains was too quiet for me, and I needed more adventure, so I left it all behind.
And your friend? The one who taught you how to skip stones?
That ended horribly. Calamity was mad at me for wanting to leave . . .
. . . told me to never come back, and I haven't seen her since.
WHOA!
MORRY!

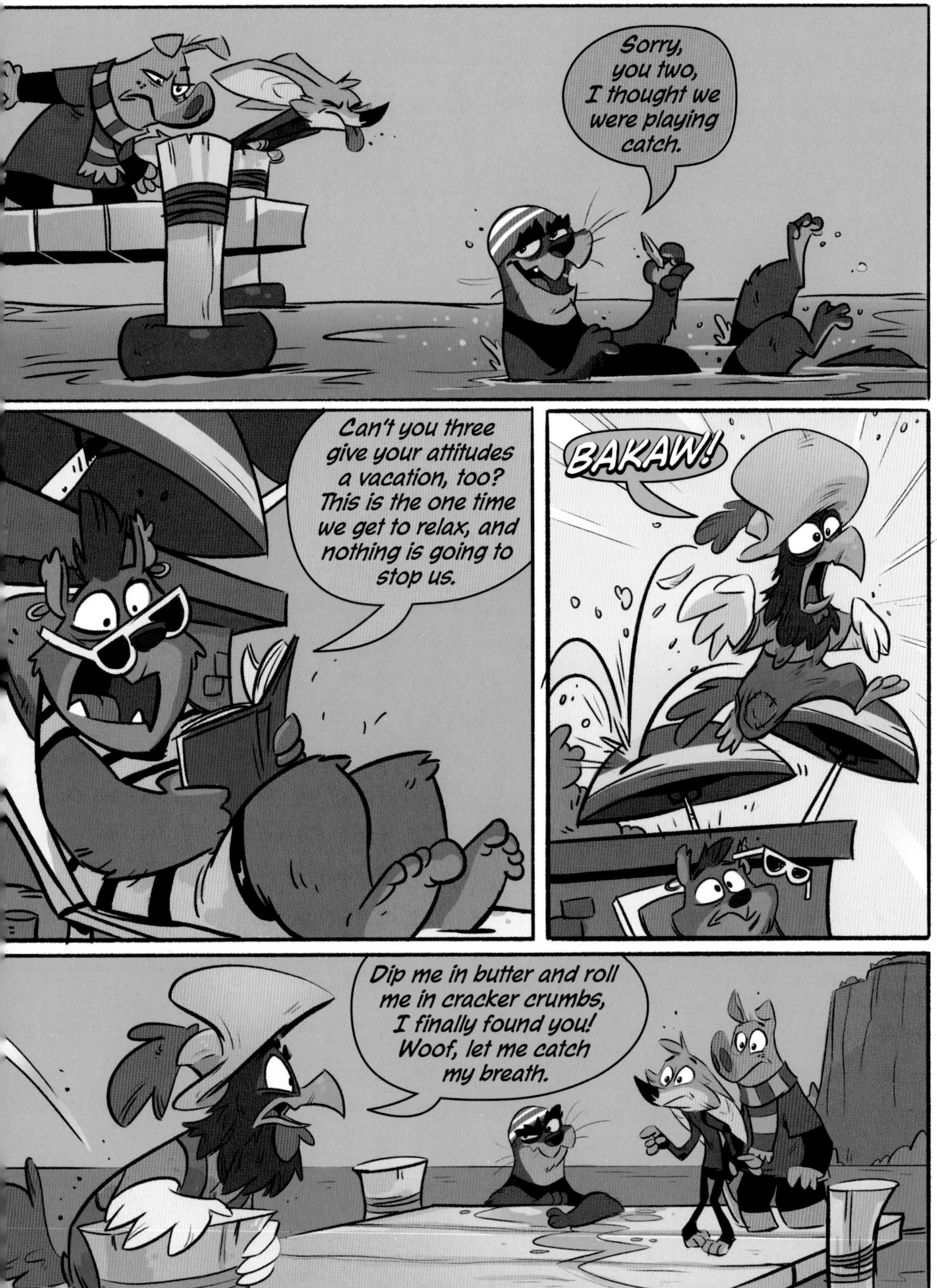
Sorry, you two, I thought we were playing catch.
Can't you three give your attitudes a vacation, too? This is the one time we get to relax, and nothing is going to stop us.
BAKAW!
Dip me in butter and roll me in cracker crumbs, I finally found you! Woof, let me catch my breath.

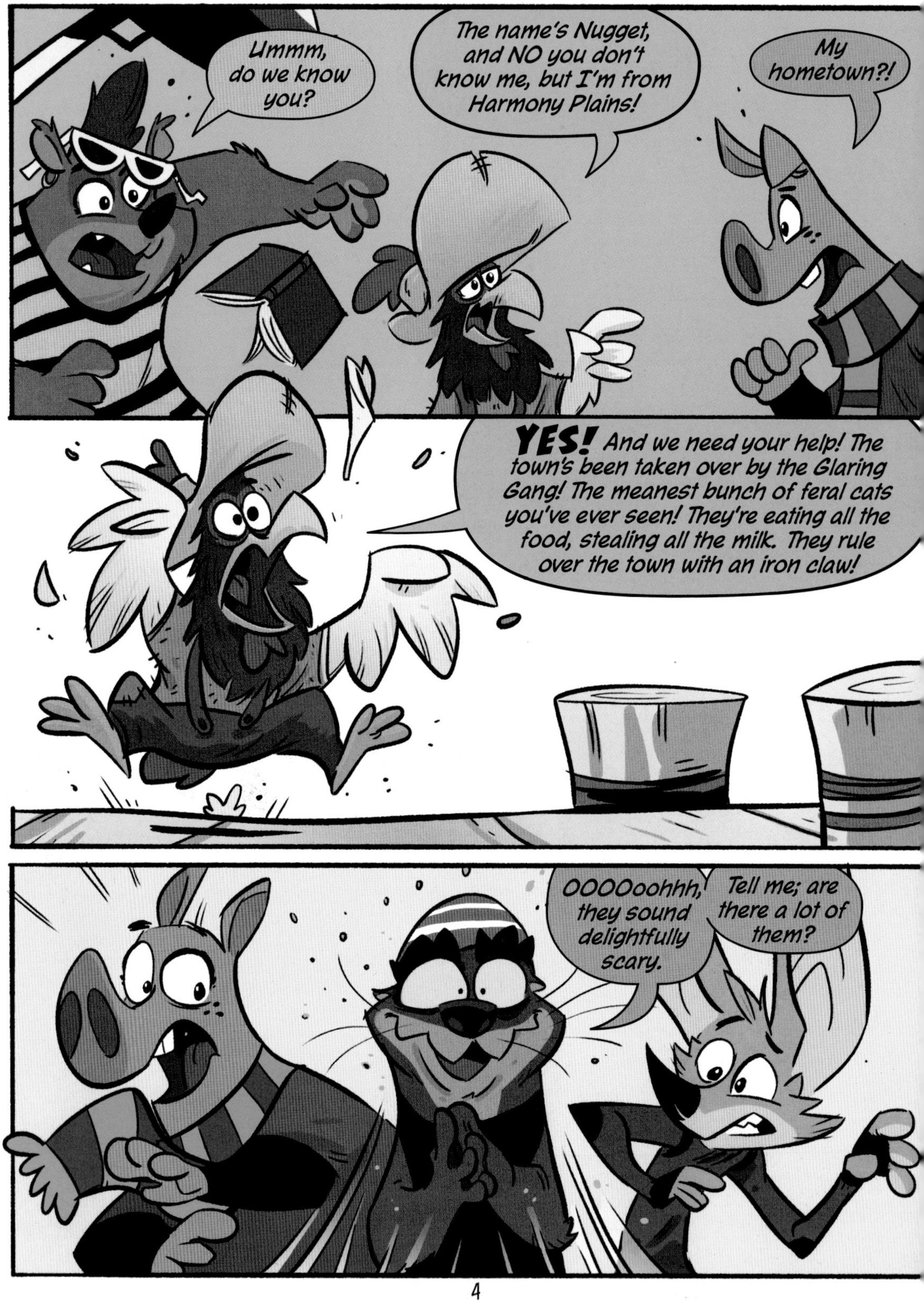
Ummm, do we know you?
The name's Nugget, and NO you don't know me, but I'm from Harmony Plains!
My hometown?!
YES! And we need your help! The town's been taken over by the Glaring Gang! The meanest bunch of feral cats you've ever seen! They're eating all the food, stealing all the milk. They rule over the town with an iron claw!
OOOOoohhh, they sound delightfully scary.
Tell me; are there a lot of them?

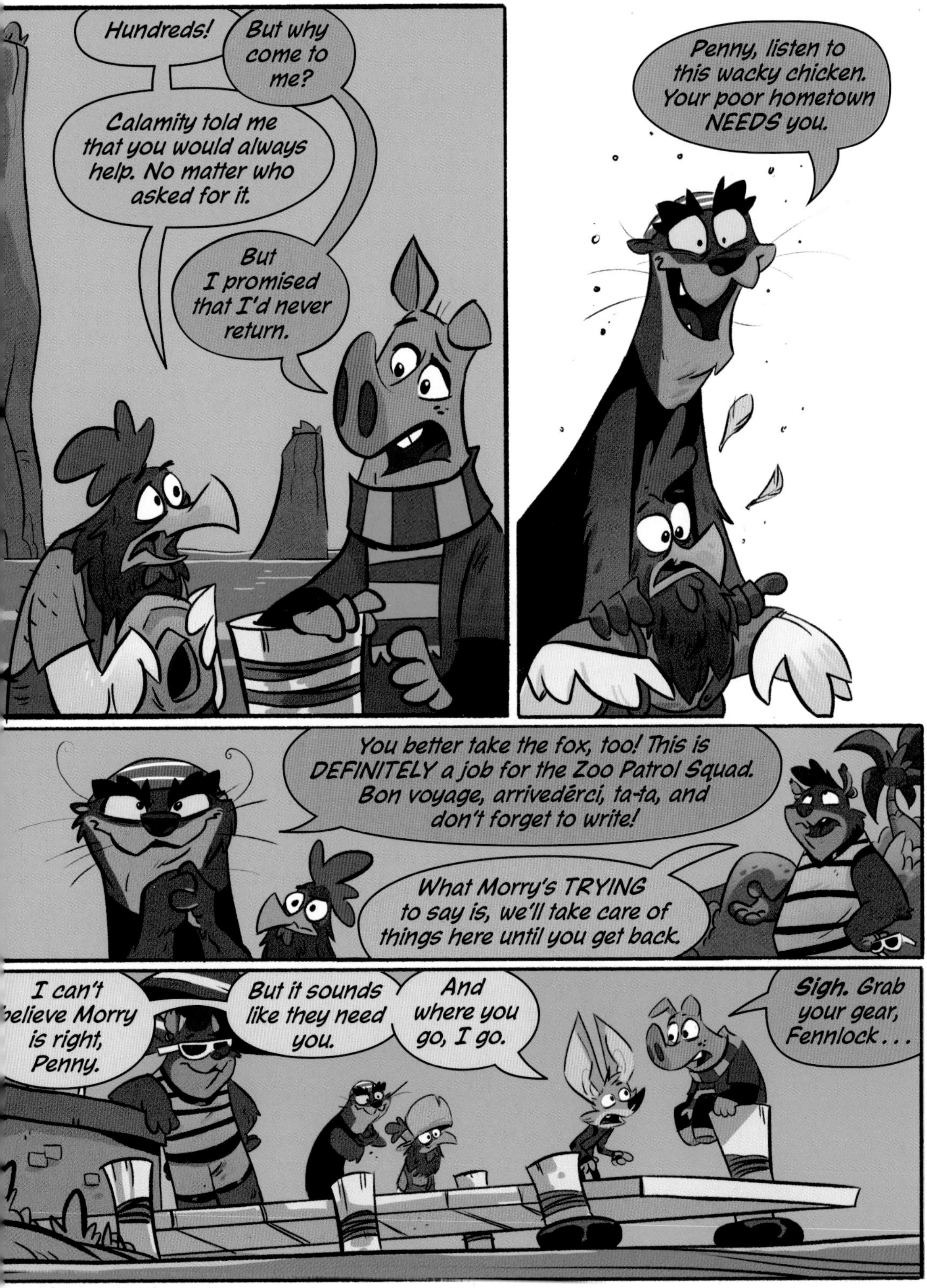
Hundreds!
But why come to me?
Calamity told me that you would always help. No matter who asked for it.
But I promised that I'd never return.
Penny, listen to this wacky chicken. Your poor hometown NEEDS you.
You better take the fox, too! This is DEFINITELY a job for the Zoo Patrol Squad. Bon voyage, arrivedérci, ta-ta, and don't forget to write!
What Morry's TRYING to say is, we'll take care of things here until you get back.
I can't believe Morry is right, Penny.
But it sounds like they need you.
And where you go, I go.
Sigh. Grab your gear, Fennlock . . .

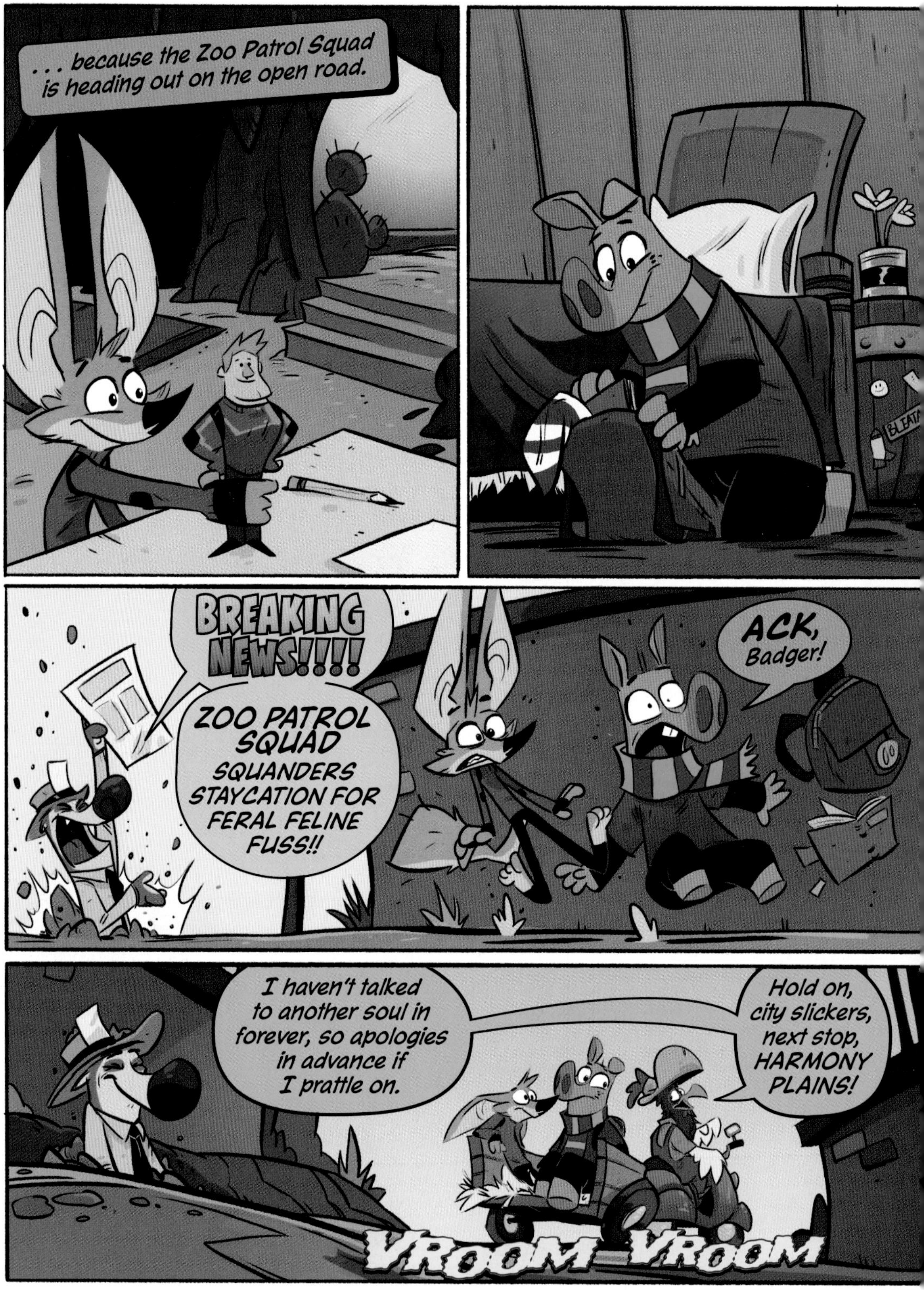
. . . because the Zoo Patrol Squad is heading out on the open road.
BLEAT
BREAKING NEWS!!!!
ZOO PATROL SQUAD SQUANDERS STAYCATION FOR FERAL FELINE FUSS!!
ACK, Badger!
I haven't talked to another soul in forever, so apologies in advance if I prattle on.
Hold on, city slickers, next stop, HARMONY PLAINS!
VROOM VROOM

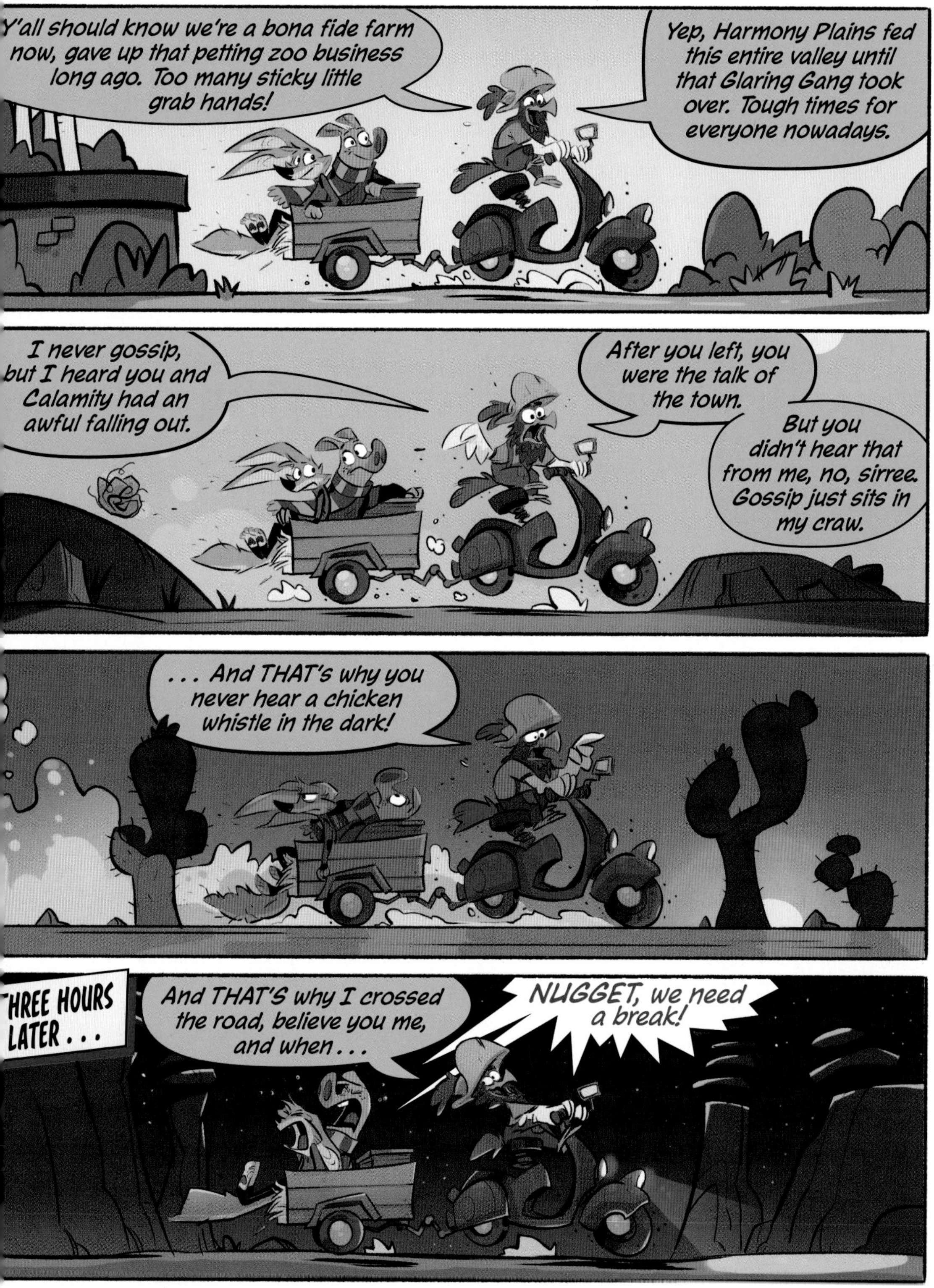
Y'all should know we're a bona fide farm now, gave up that petting zoo business long ago. Too many sticky little grab hands!
Yep, Harmony Plains fed this entire valley until that Glaring Gang took over. Tough times for everyone nowadays.
I never gossip, but I heard you and Calamity had an awful falling out.
After you left, you were the talk of the town.
But you didn't hear that from me, no, sirree. Gossip just sits in my craw.
. . . And THAT's why you never hear a chicken whistle in the dark!
THREE HOURS LATER . . .
And THAT'S why I crossed the road, believe you me, and when . . .
NUGGET, we need a break!

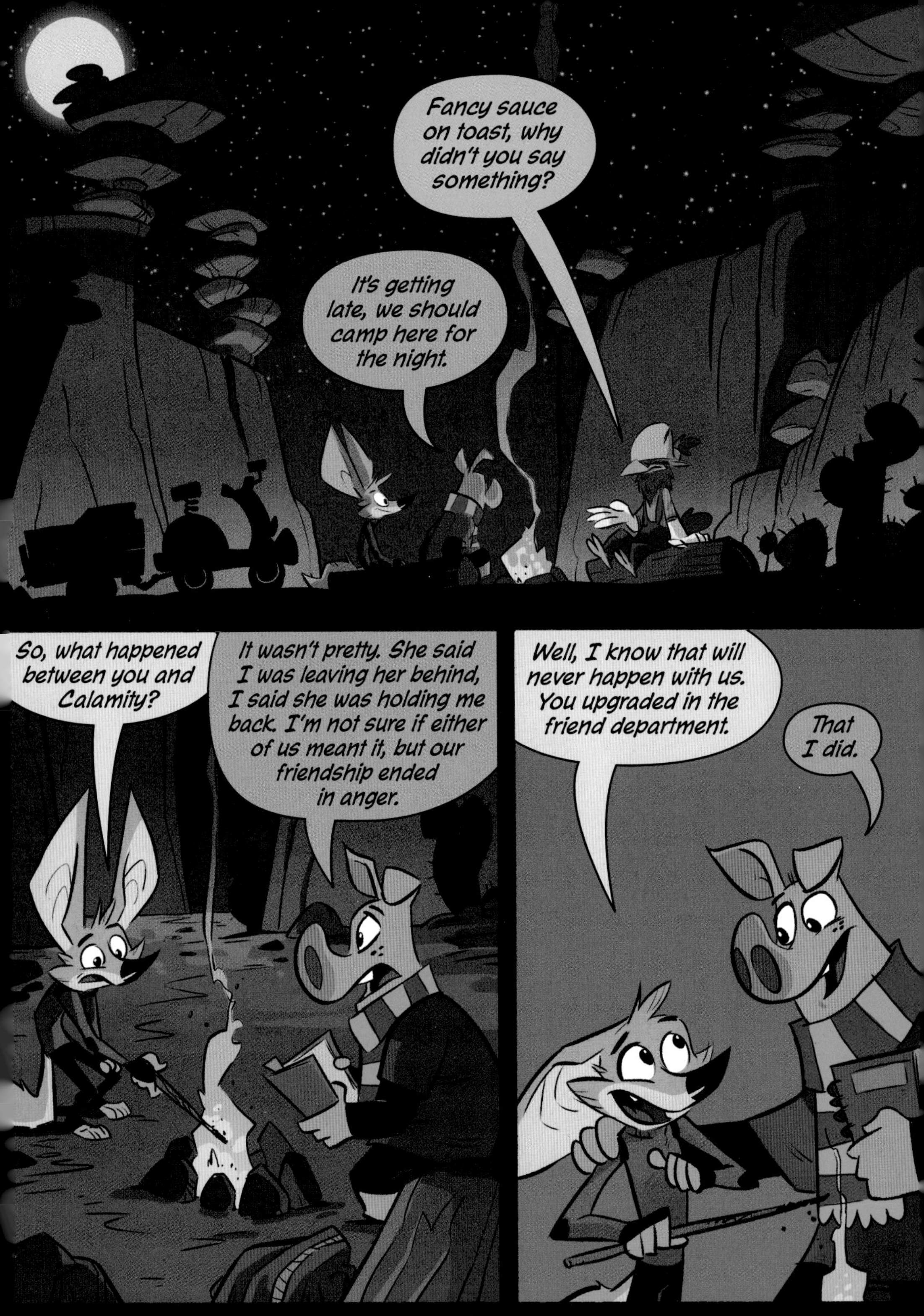
It's getting late, we should camp here for the night.
Fancy sauce on toast, why didn't you say something?
So, what happened between you and Calamity?
It wasn't pretty. She said I was leaving her behind, I said she was holding me back. I'm not sure if either of us meant it, but our friendship ended in anger.
Well, I know that will never happen with us. You upgraded in the friend department.
That I did.

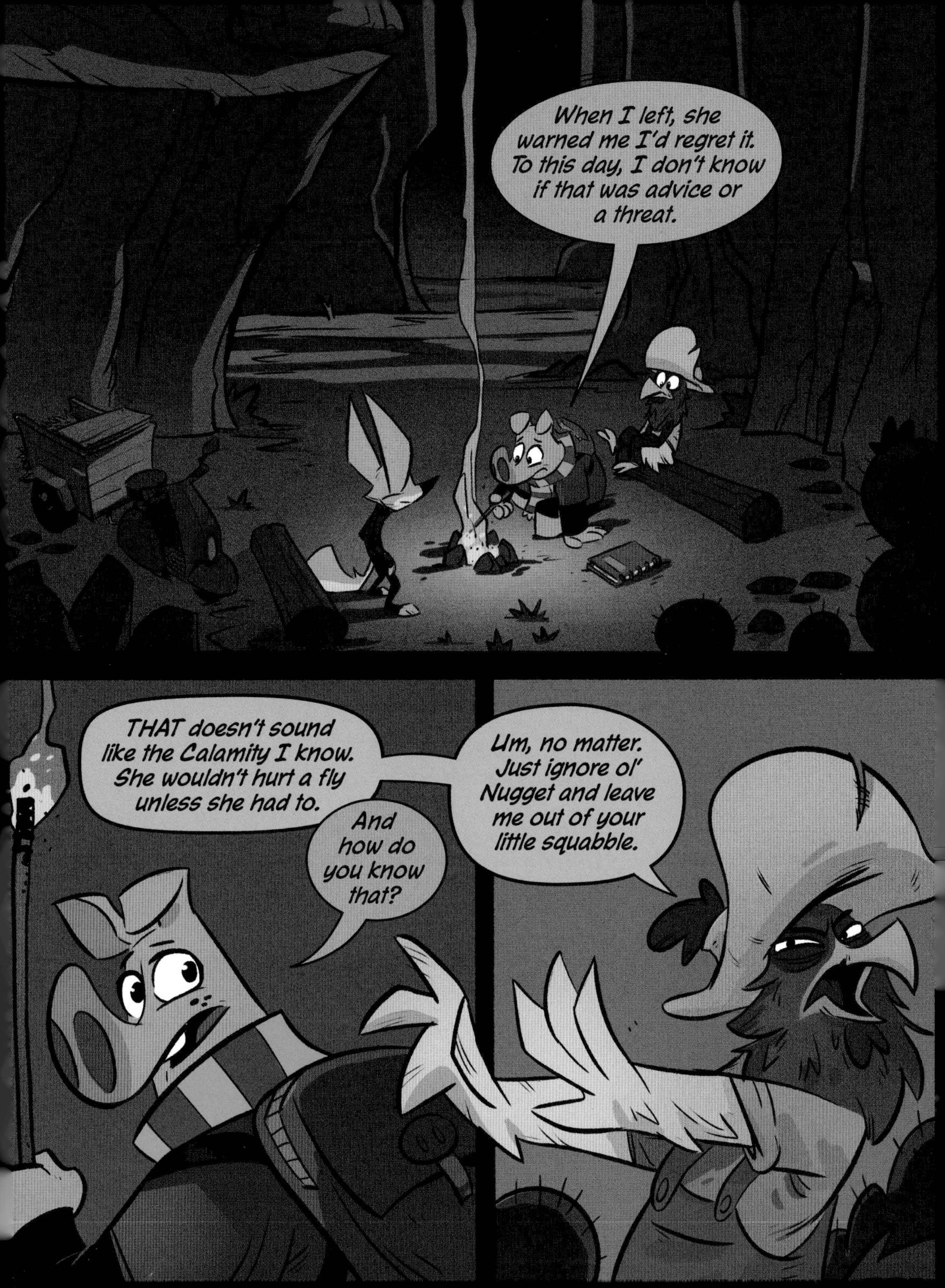
When I left, she warned me I'd regret it. To this day, I don't know if that was advice or a threat.
THAT doesn't sound like the Calamity I know. She wouldn't hurt a fly unless she had to.
And how do you know that?
Um, no matter. Just ignore ol' Nugget and leave me out of your little squabble.

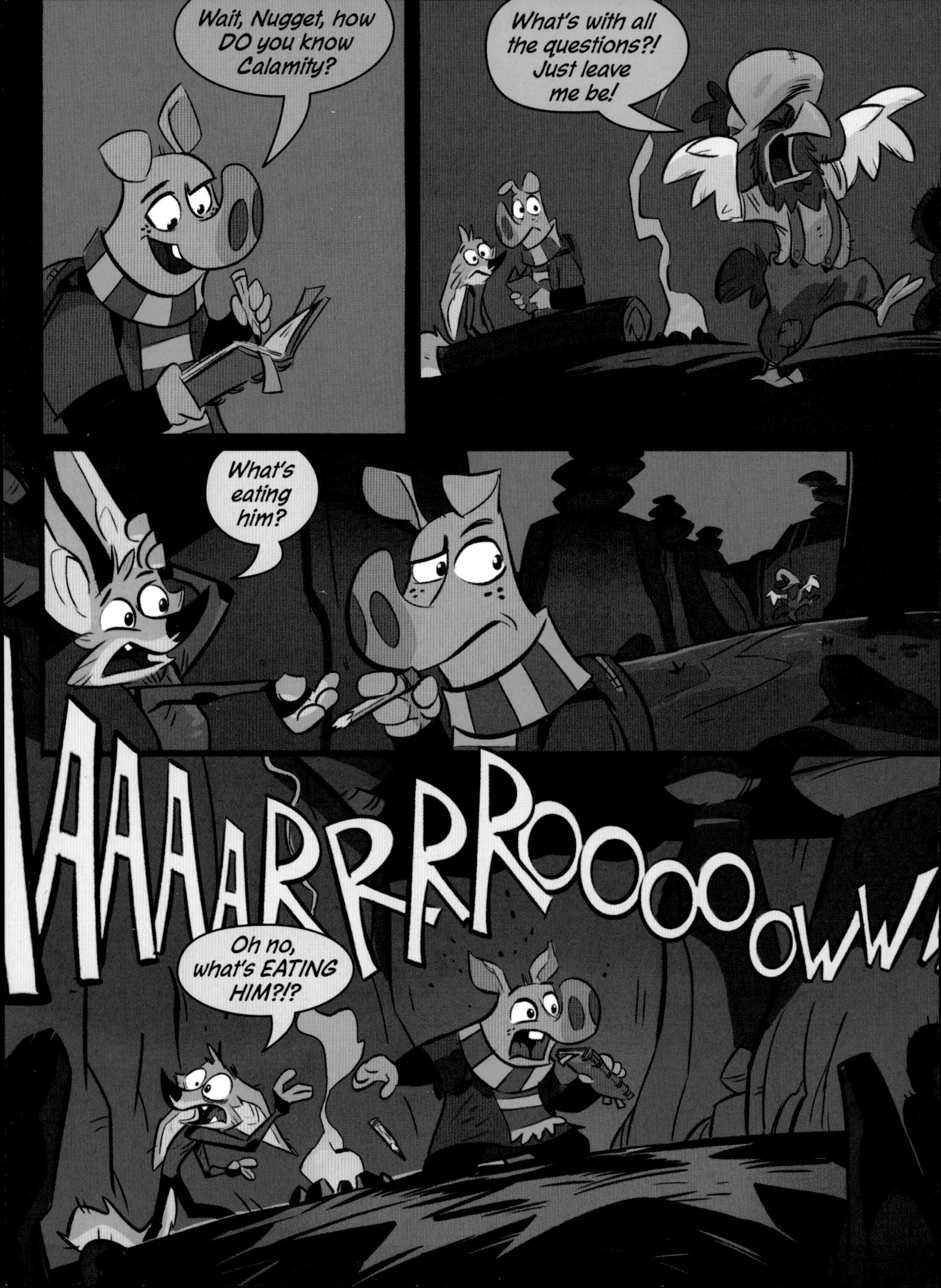
Wait, Nugget, how DO you know Calamity?
What's with all the questions?! Just leave me be!
What's eating him?
AAAARRRROOOOOOWW
Oh no, what's EATING HIM?!?

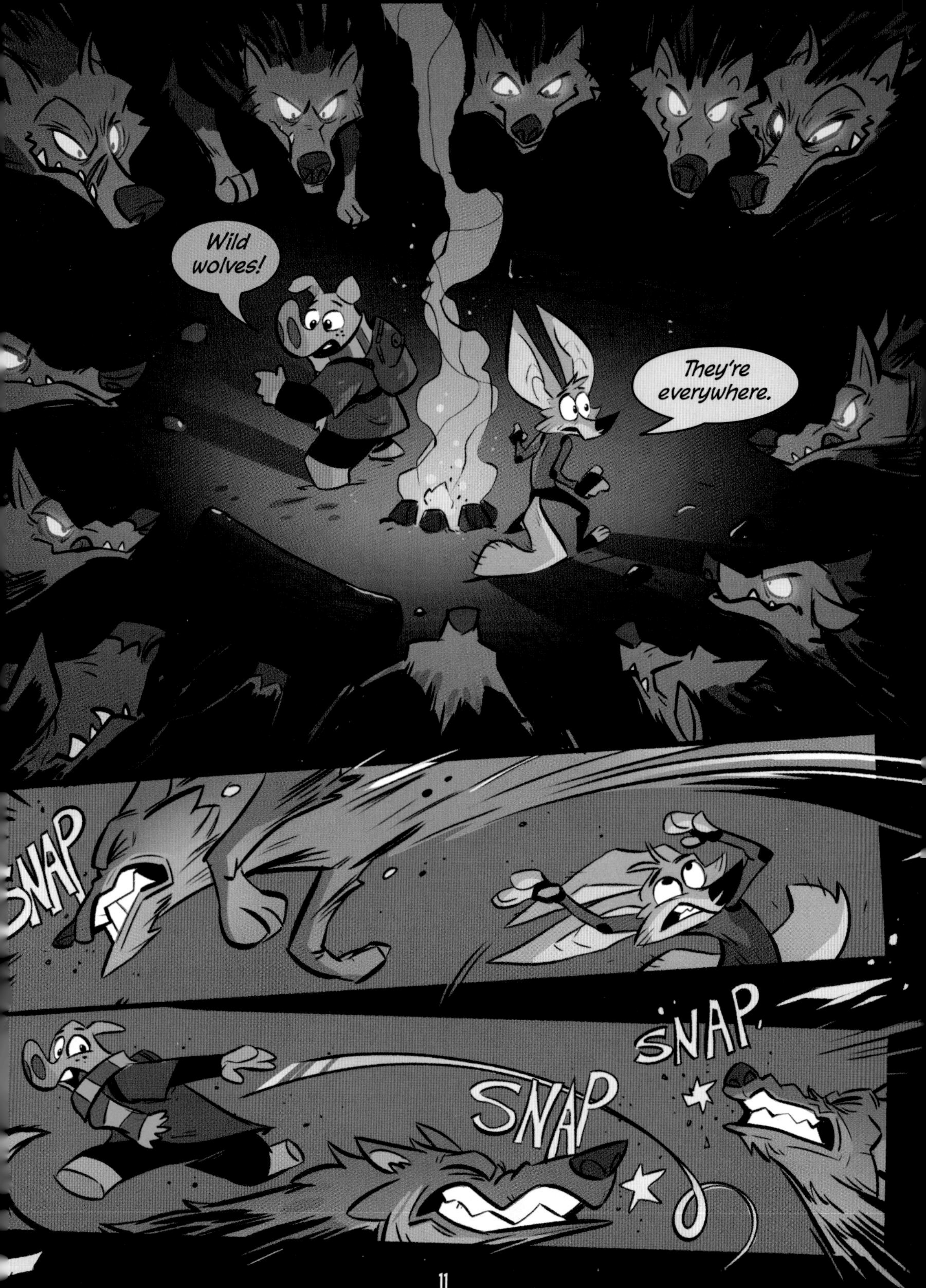
Wild wolves!
They're everywhere.
SNAP
SNAP
SNAP

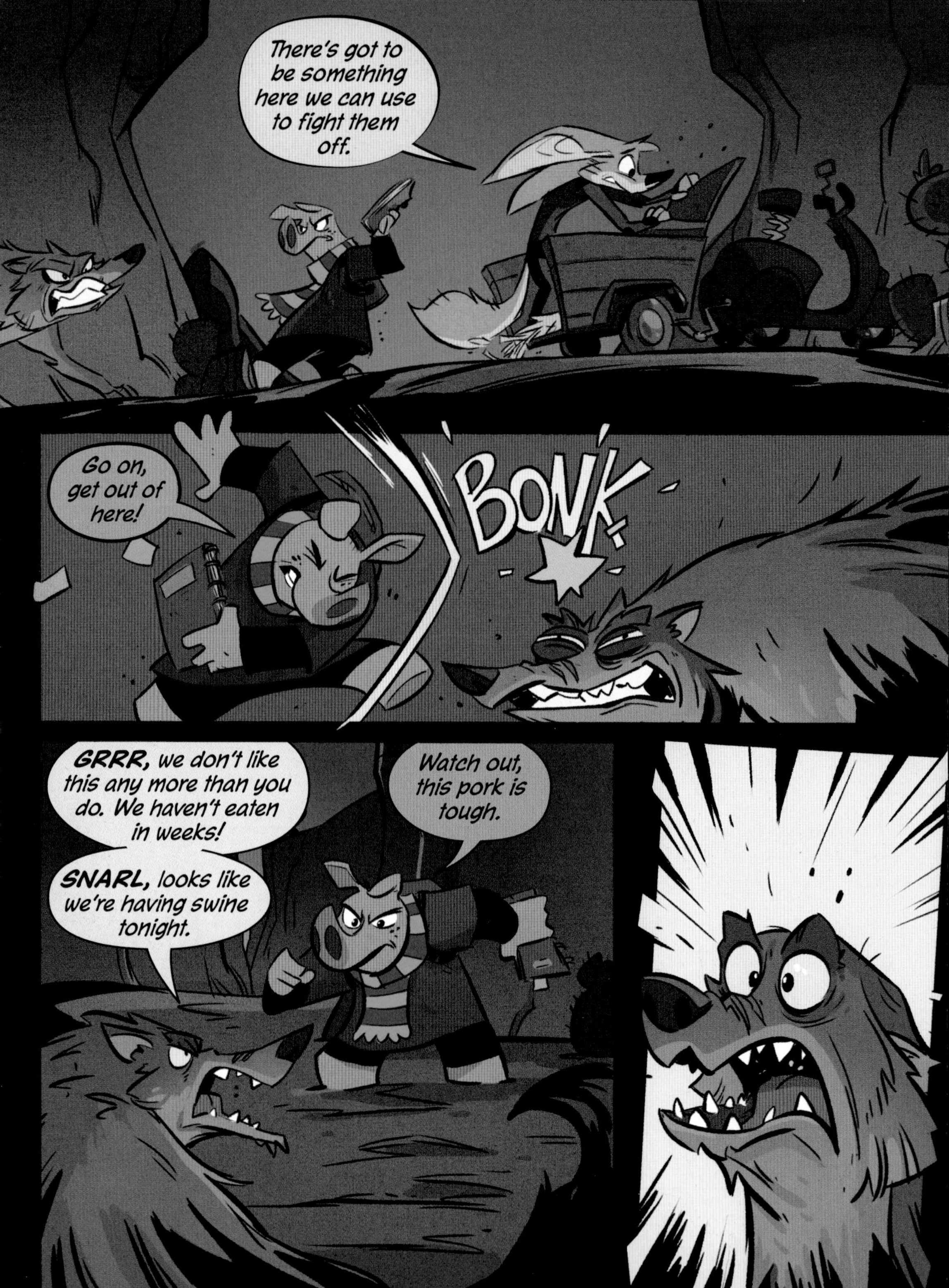
There's got to be something here we can use to fight them off.
Go on, get out of here!
BONK
GRRR, we don't like this any more than you do. We haven't eaten in weeks!
SNARL, looks like we're having swine tonight.
Watch out, this pork is tough.

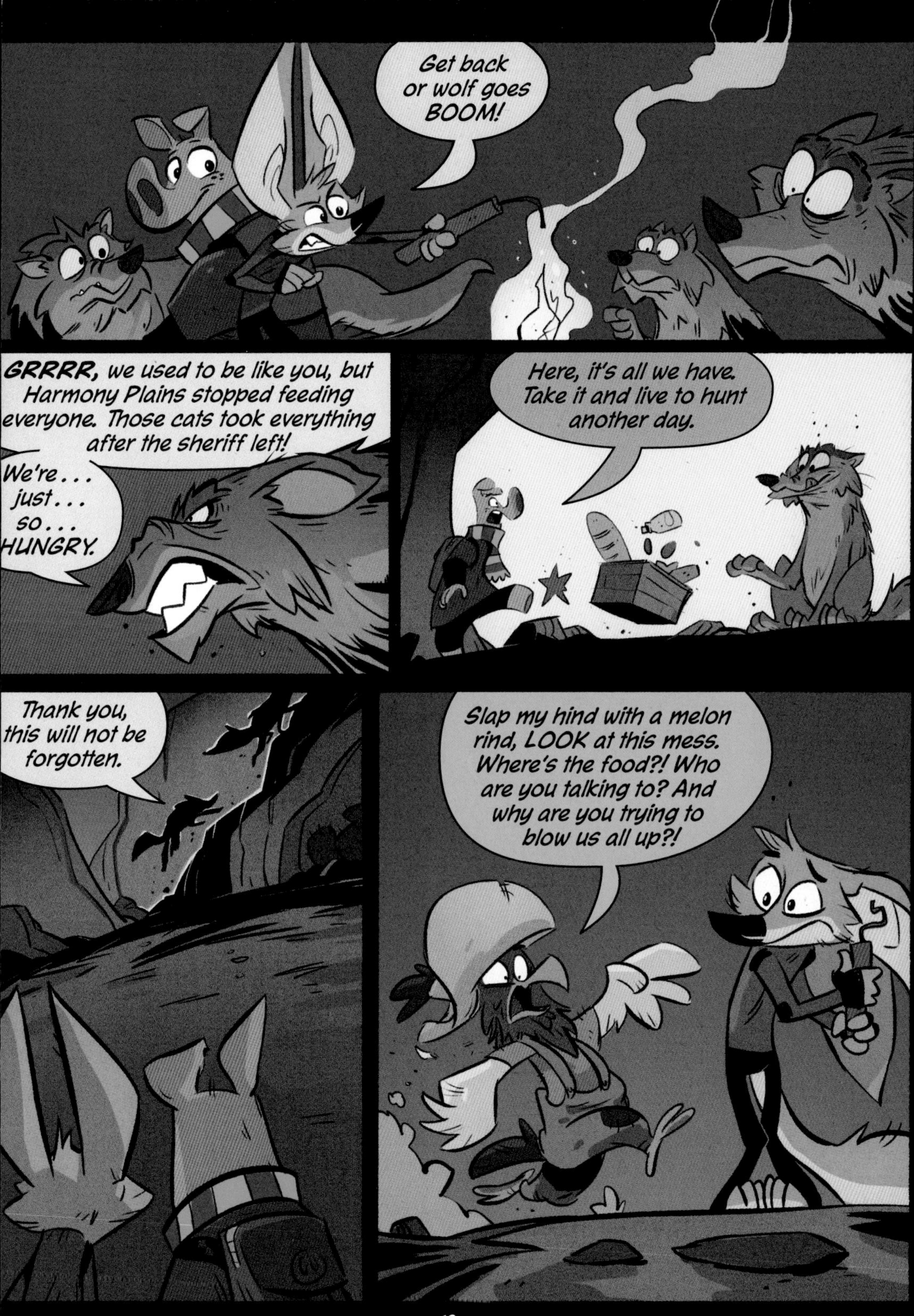
Get back or wolf goes BOOM!
GRRRR, we used to be like you, but Harmony Plains stopped feeding everyone. Those cats took everything after the sheriff left!
We're... just... so... HUNGRY.
Here, it's all we have. Take it and live to hunt another day.
Thank you, this will not be forgotten.
Slap my hind with a melon rind, LOOK at this mess. Where's the food?! Who are you talking to? And why are you trying to blow us all up?!

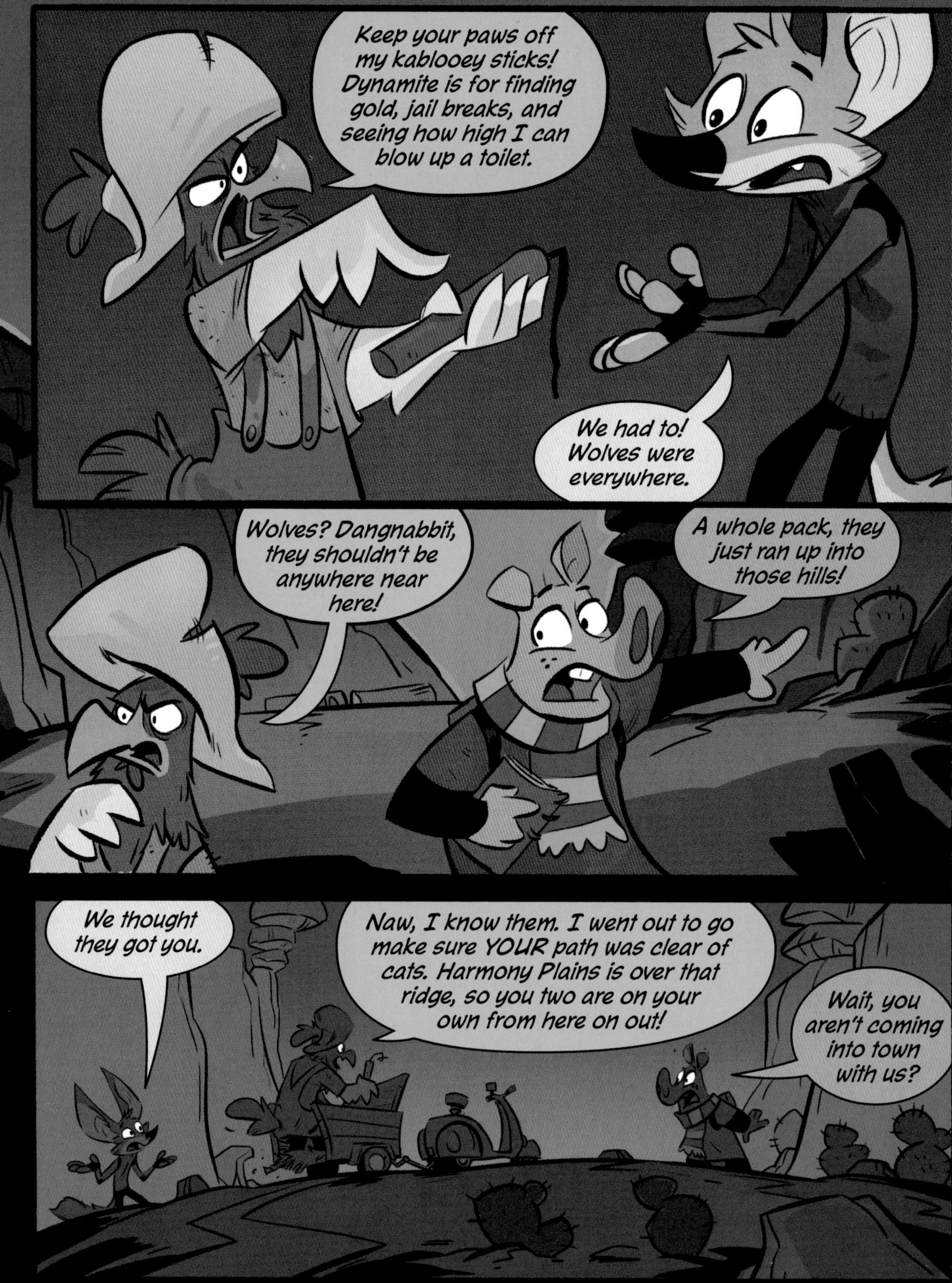

Keep your paws off my kablooey sticks! Dynamite is for finding gold, jail breaks, and seeing how high I can blow up a toilet.
We had to! Wolves were everywhere.
Wolves? Dangnabbit, they shouldn't be anywhere near here!
A whole pack, they just ran up into those hills!
We thought they got you.
Naw, I know them. I went out to go make sure YOUR path was clear of cats. Harmony Plains is over that ridge, so you two are on your own from here on out!
Wait, you aren't coming into town with us?

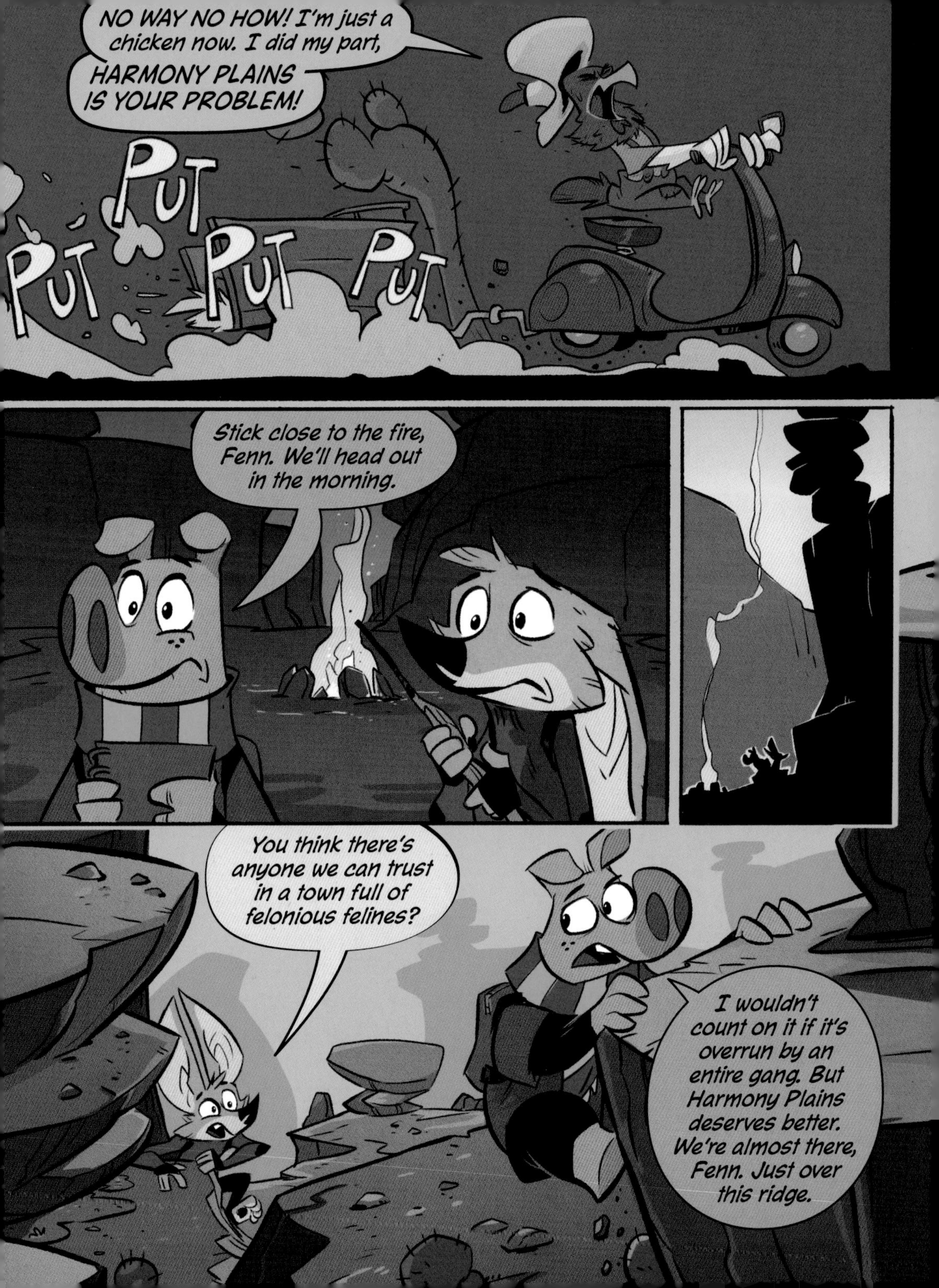
NO WAY NO HOW! I'm just a chicken now. I did my part,
HARMONY PLAINS IS YOUR PROBLEM!
PUT PUT PUT PUT PUT
Stick close to the fire, Fenn. We'll head out in the morning.
You think there's anyone we can trust in a town full of felonious felines?
I wouldn't count on it if it's overrun by an entire gang. But Harmony Plains deserves better. We're almost there, Fenn. Just over this ridge.

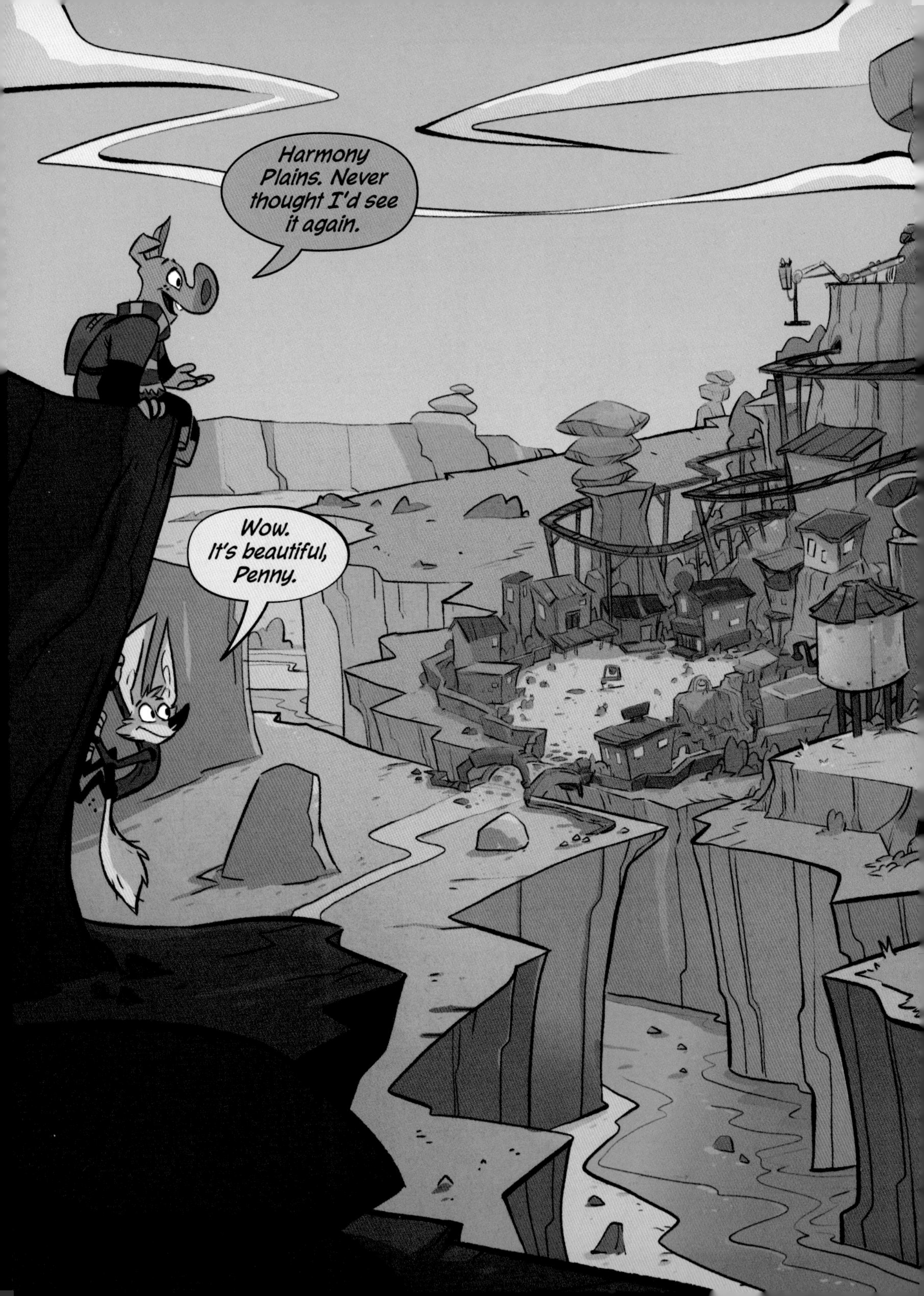
Harmony Plains. Never thought I'd see it again.
Wow. It's beautiful, Penny.

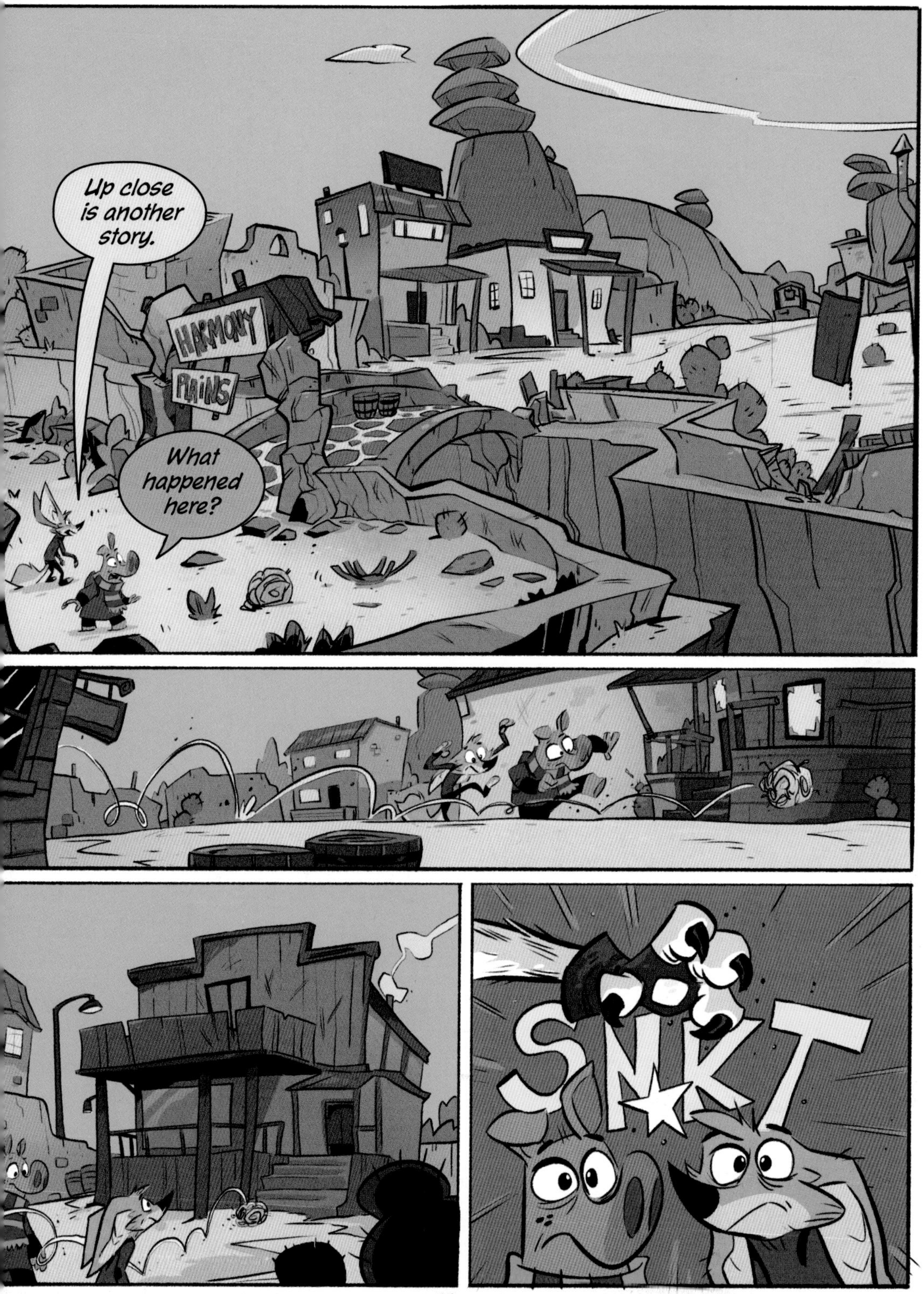
Up close is another story.
HARMONY
PLAINS
What happened here?
SNKT

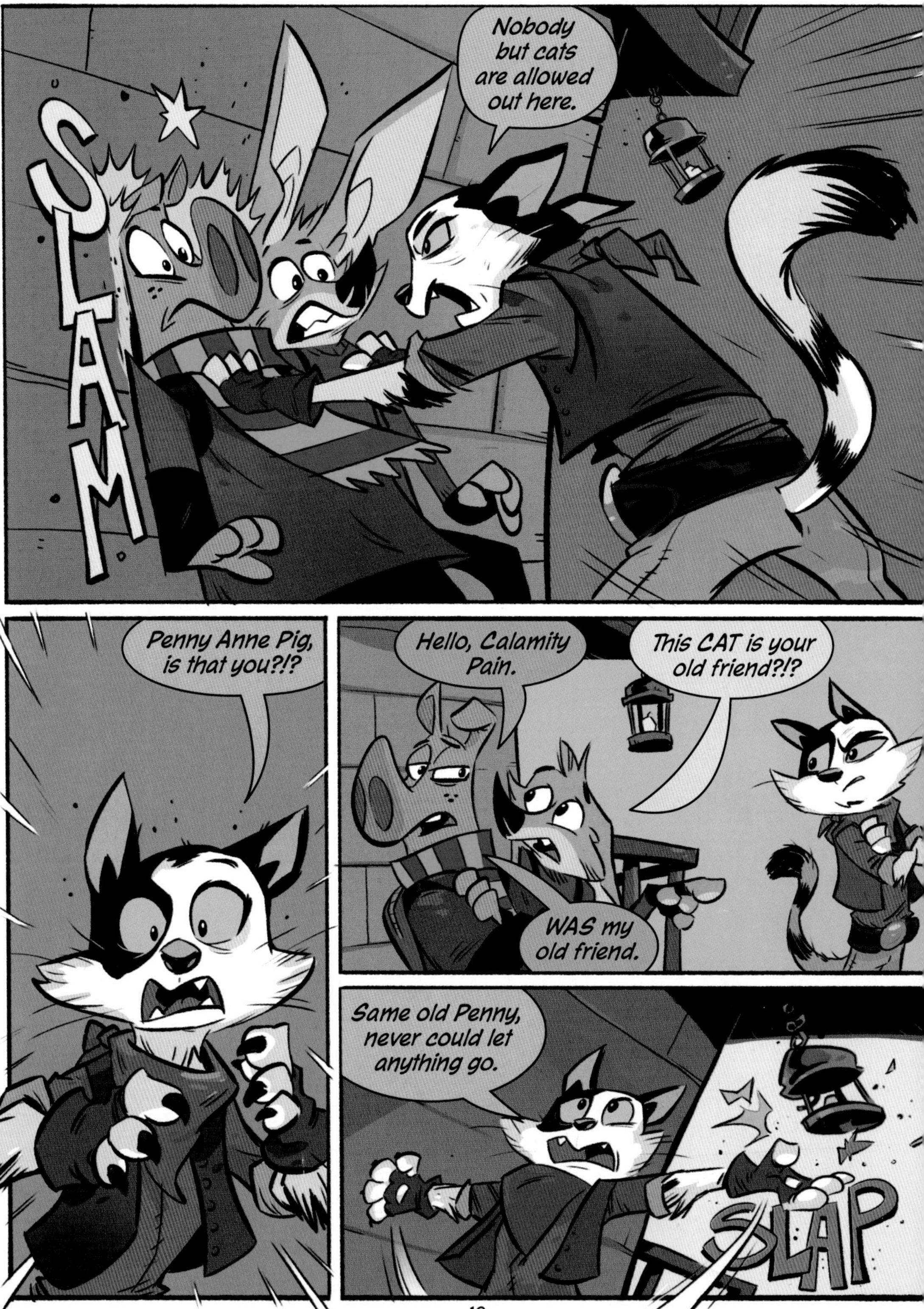

Nobody but cats are allowed out here.
SLAM
Penny Anne Pig, is that you?!?
Hello, Calamity Pain.
This CAT is your old friend?!?
WAS my old friend.
Same old Penny, never could let anything go.
SLAP

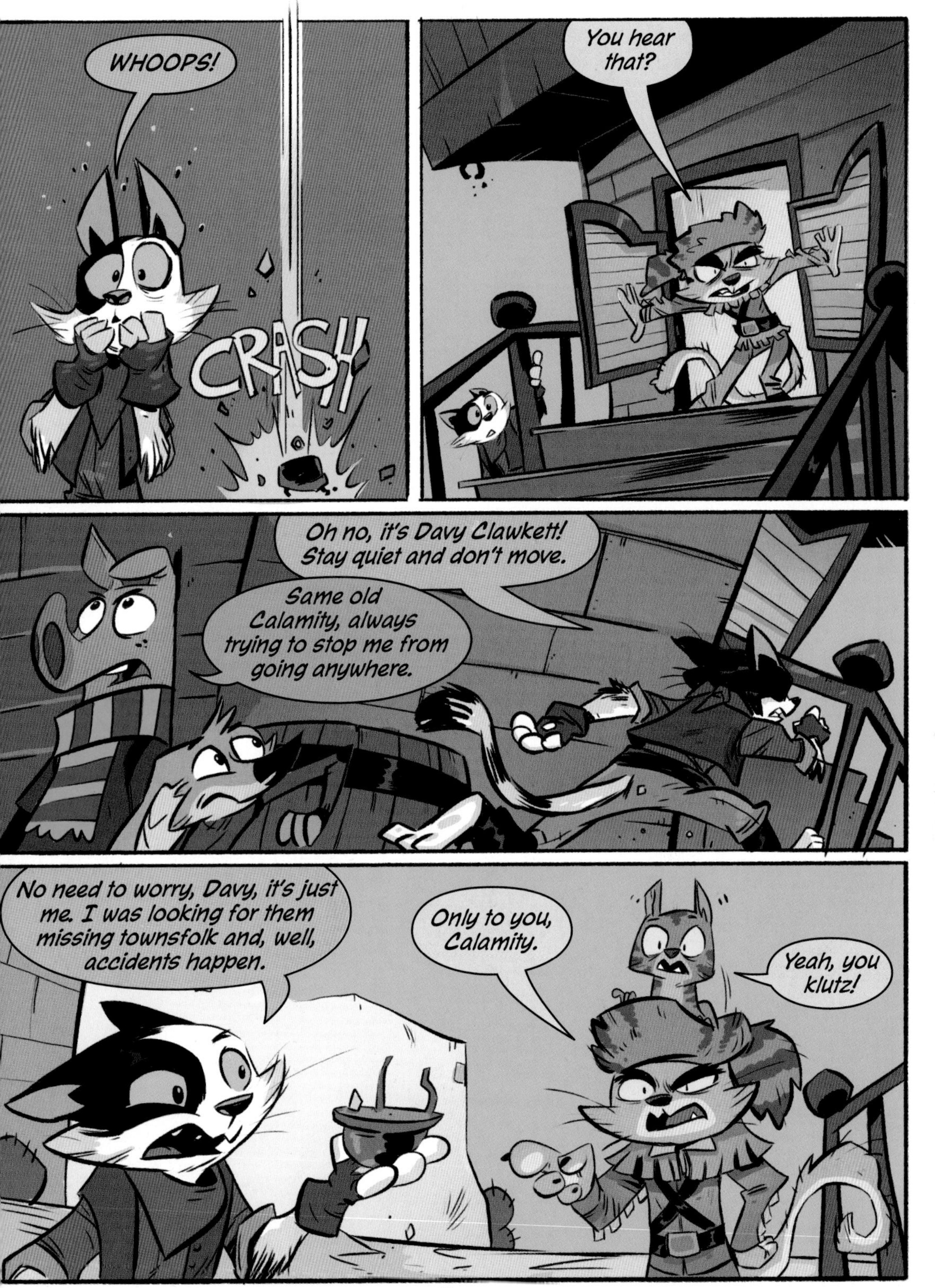
WHOOPS!
CRASH
You hear that?
Oh no, it's Davy Clawkett! Stay quiet and don't move.
Same old Calamity, always trying to stop me from going anywhere.
No need to worry, Davy, it's just me. I was looking for them missing townsfolk and, well, accidents happen.
Only to you, Calamity.
Yeah, you klutz!

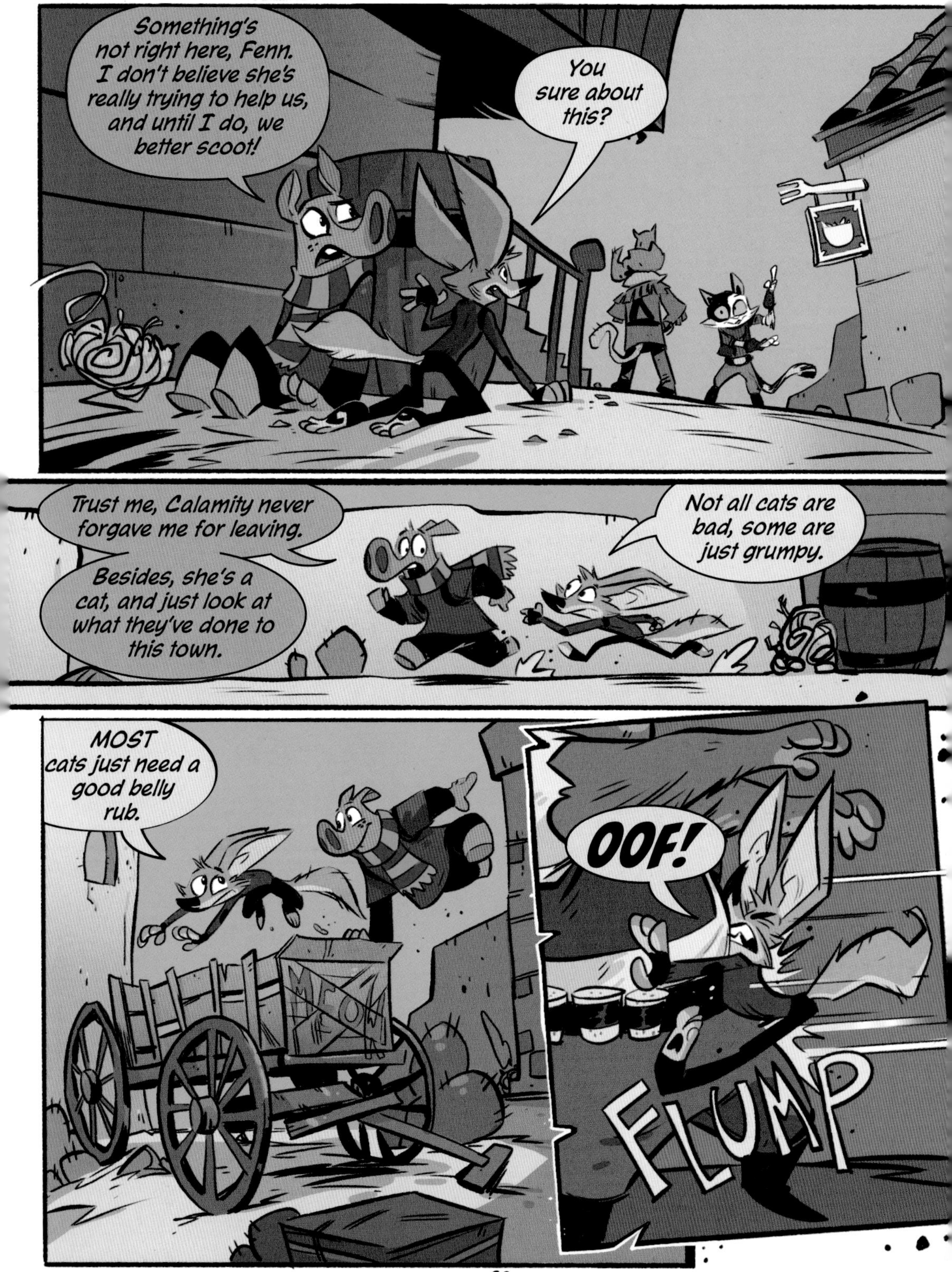
Something's not right here, Fenn. I don't believe she's really trying to help us, and until I do, we better scoot!
You sure about this?
Trust me, Calamity never forgave me for leaving.
Besides, she's a cat, and just look at what they've done to this town.
Not all cats are bad, some are just grumpy.
MOST cats just need a good belly rub.
MEOW
OOF!
FLUMP

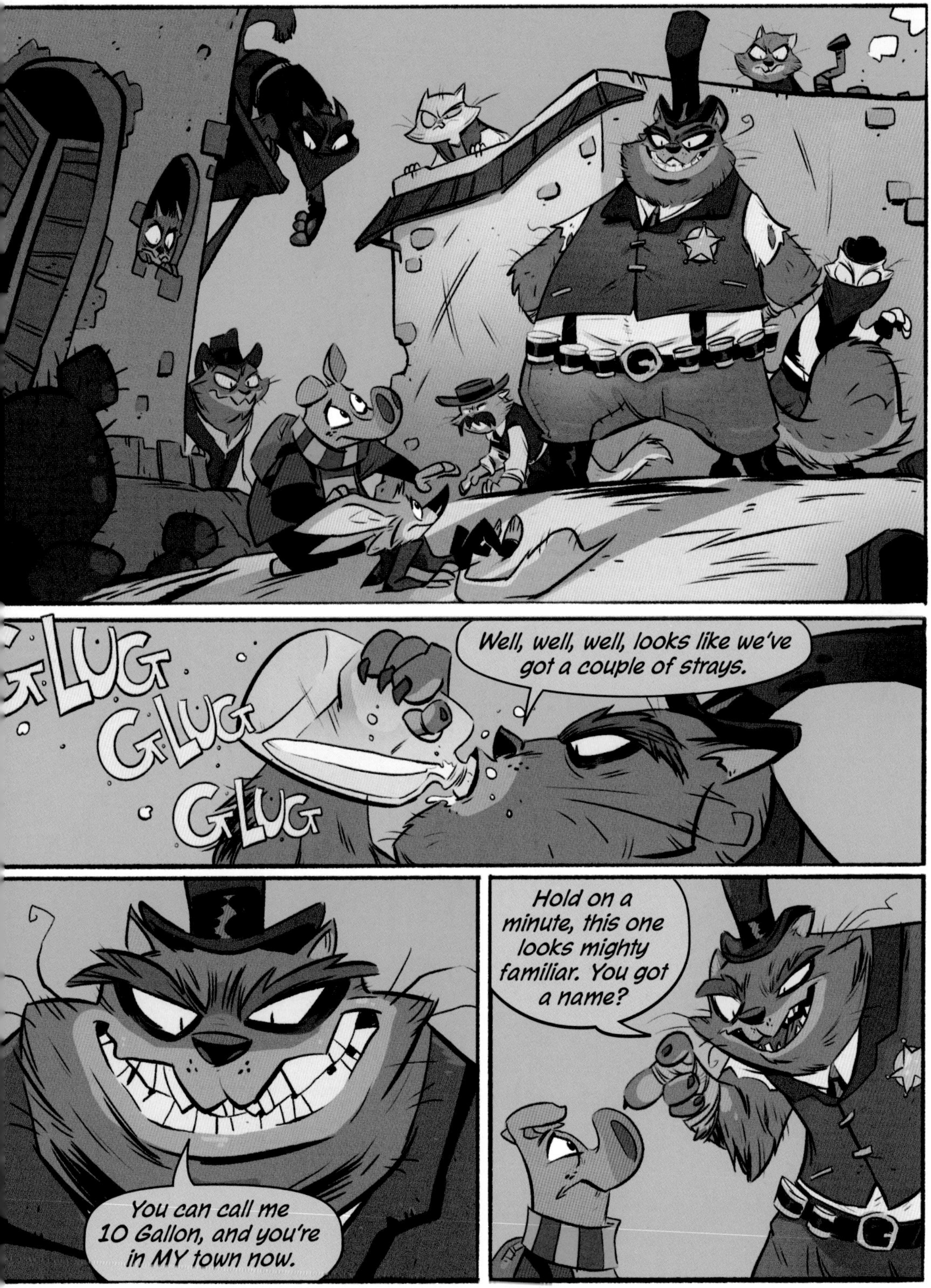
GLUG
GLUG
GLUG
Well, well, well, looks like we've got a couple of strays.
You can call me 10 Gallon, and you're in MY town now.
Hold on a minute, this one looks mighty familiar. You got a name?

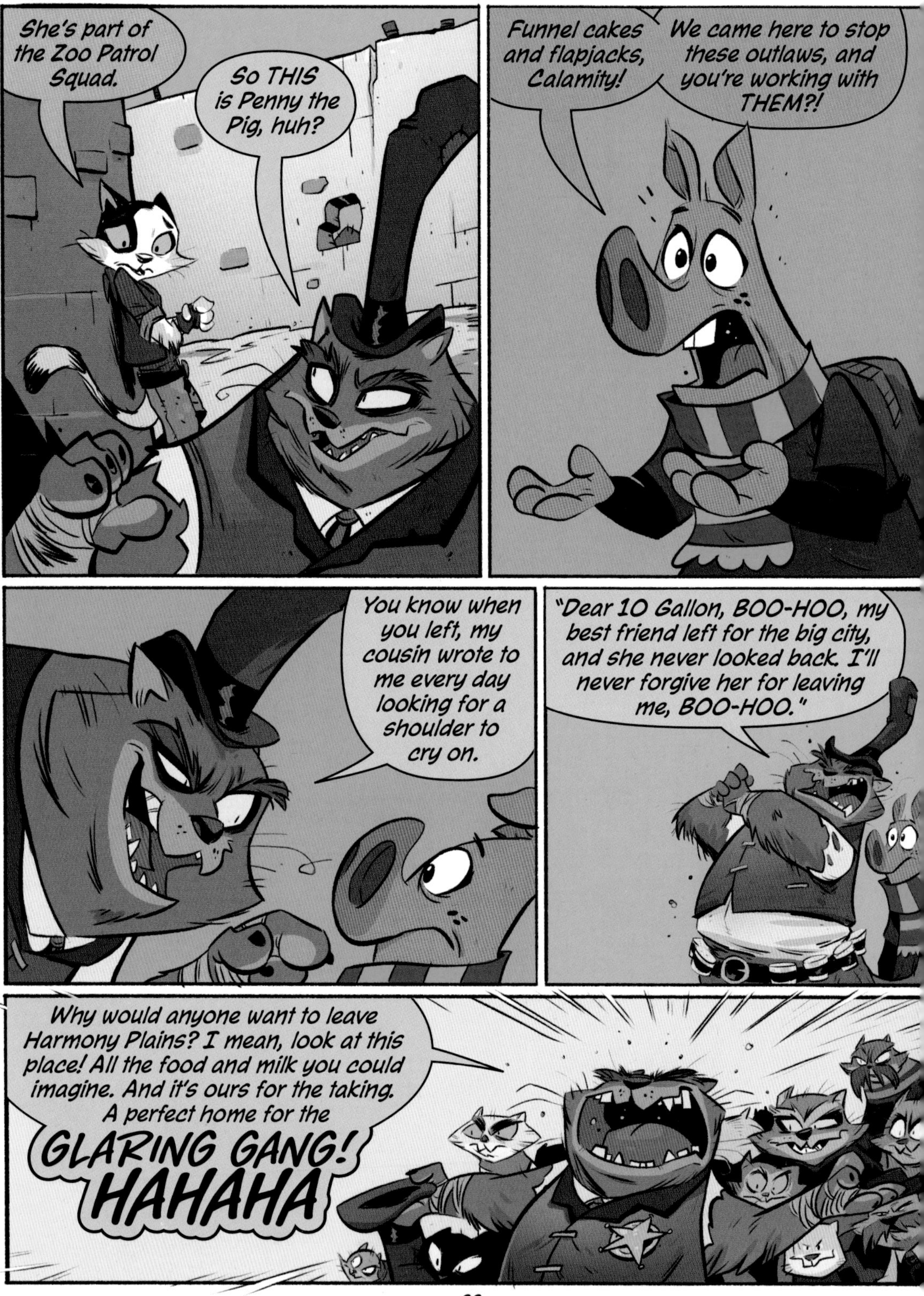
She's part of the Zoo Patrol Squad.
So THIS is Penny the Pig, huh?
Funnel cakes and flapjacks, Calamity!
We came here to stop these outlaws, and you're working with THEM?!
You know when you left, my cousin wrote to me every day looking for a shoulder to cry on.
"Dear 10 Gallon, BOO-HOO, my best friend left for the big city, and she never looked back. I'll never forgive her for leaving me, BOO-HOO."
Why would anyone want to leave Harmony Plains? I mean, look at this place! All the food and milk you could imagine. And it's ours for the taking. A perfect home for the
GLARING GANG!
HAHAHA

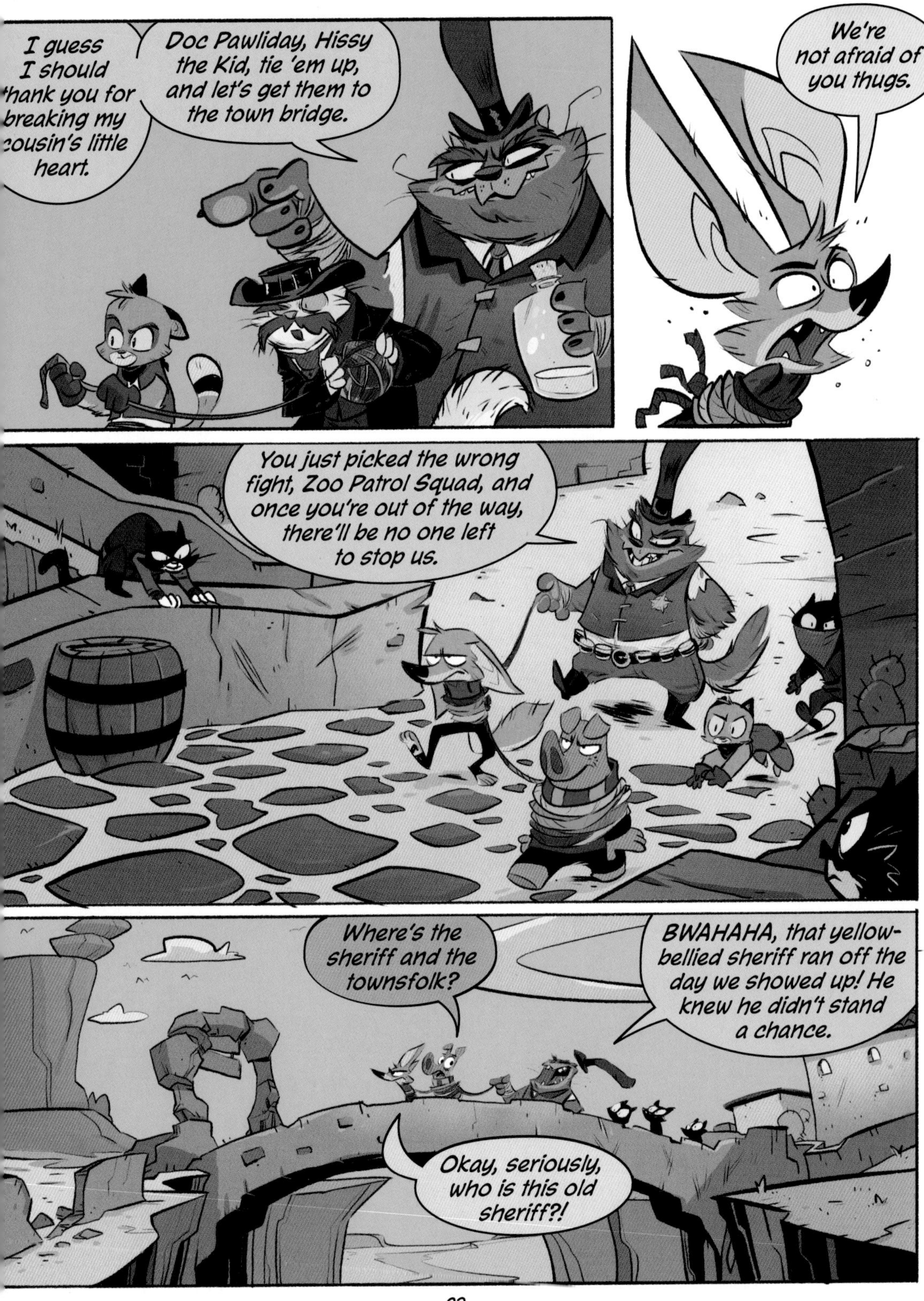

I guess I should thank you for breaking my cousin's little heart.
Doc Pawliday, Hissy the Kid, tie 'em up, and let's get them to the town bridge.
We're not afraid of you thugs.
You just picked the wrong fight, Zoo Patrol Squad, and once you're out of the way, there'll be no one left to stop us.
Where's the sheriff and the townsfolk?
BWAHAHA, that yellow-bellied sheriff ran off the day we showed up! He knew he didn't stand a chance.
Okay, seriously, who is this old sheriff?!

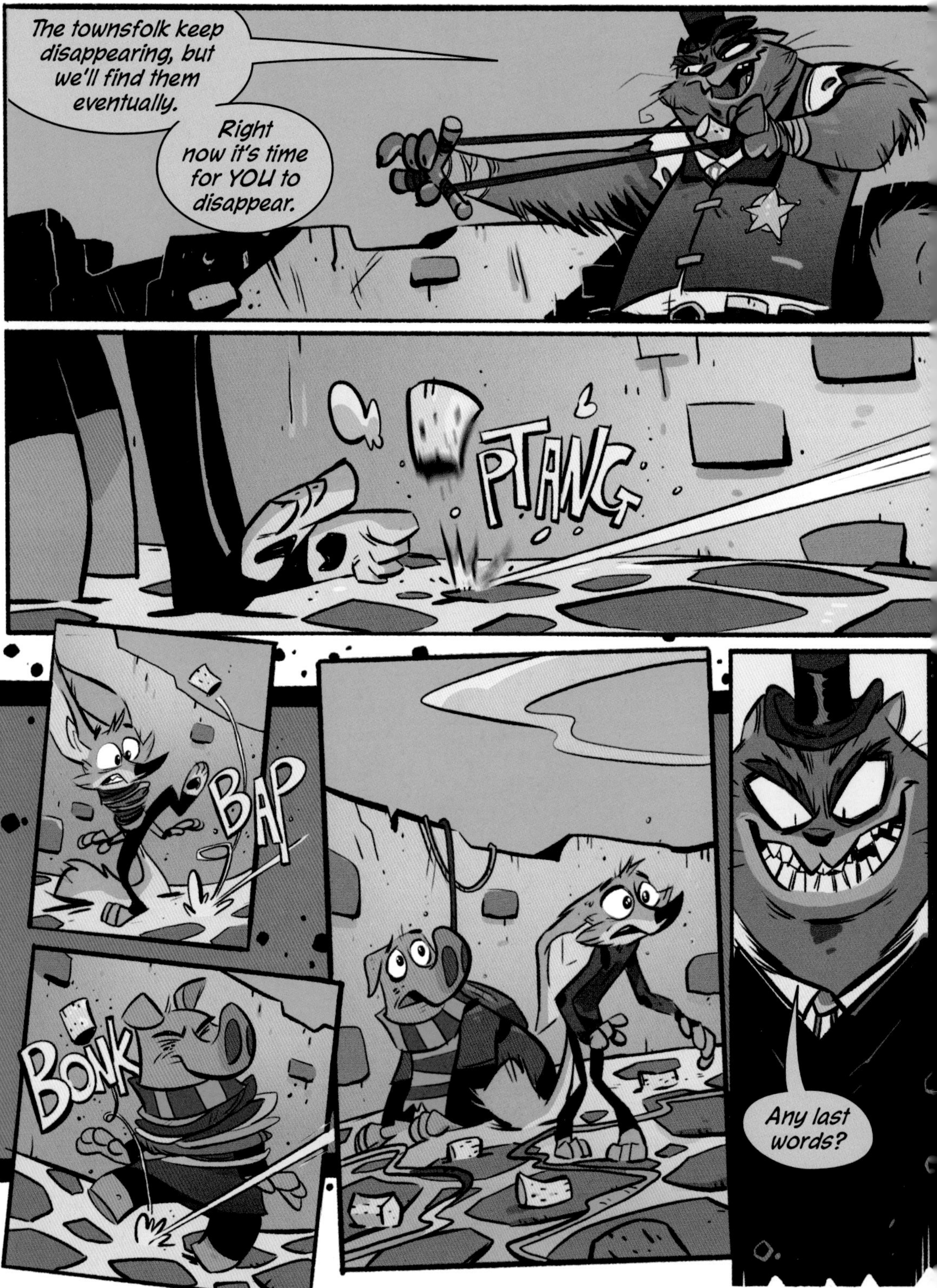
The townsfolk keep disappearing, but we'll find them eventually.
Right now it's time for YOU to disappear.
PTANG
BAP
BONK
Any last words?

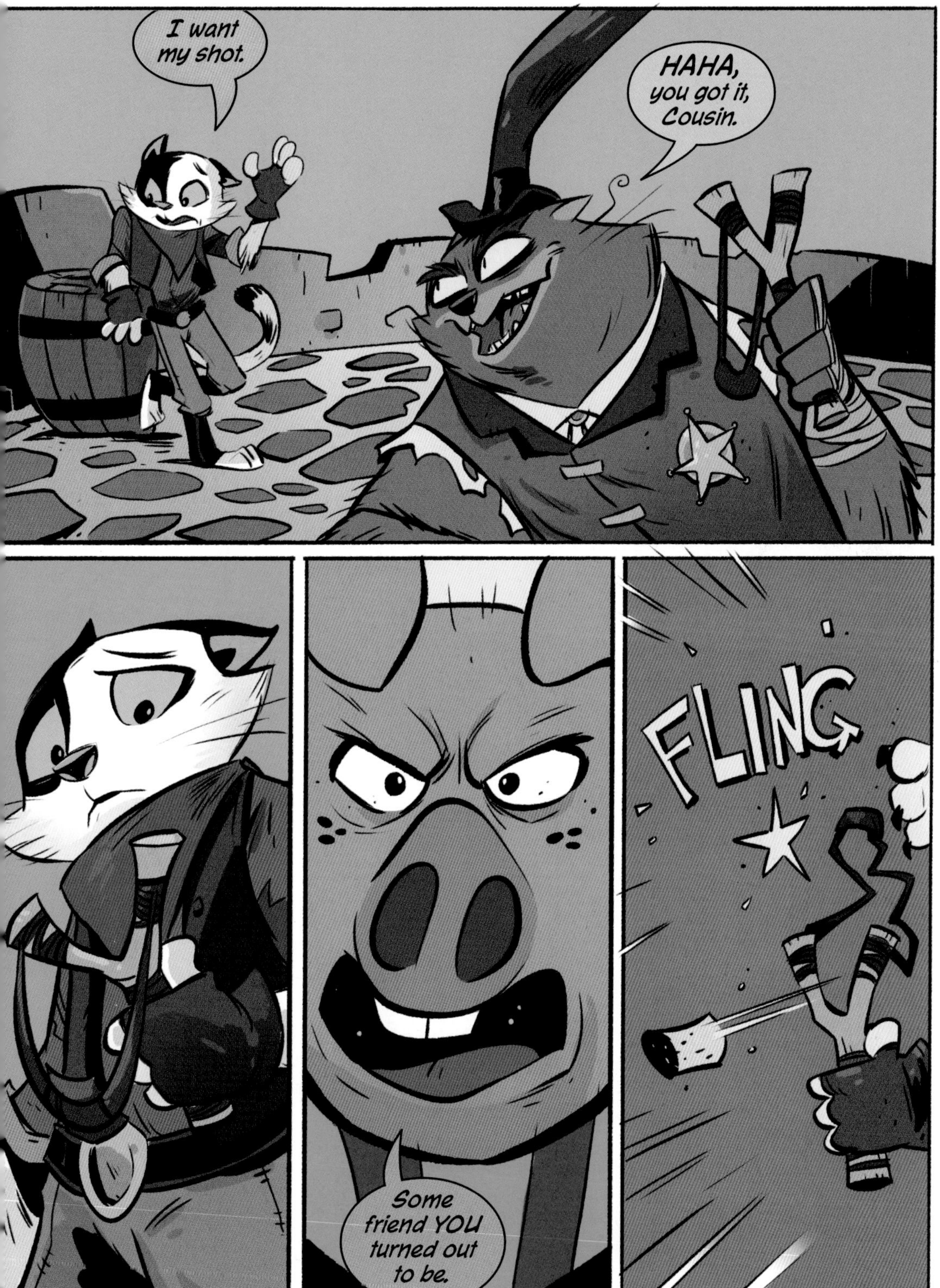
I want my shot.
HAHA, you got it, Cousin.
Some friend YOU turned out to be.
FLING

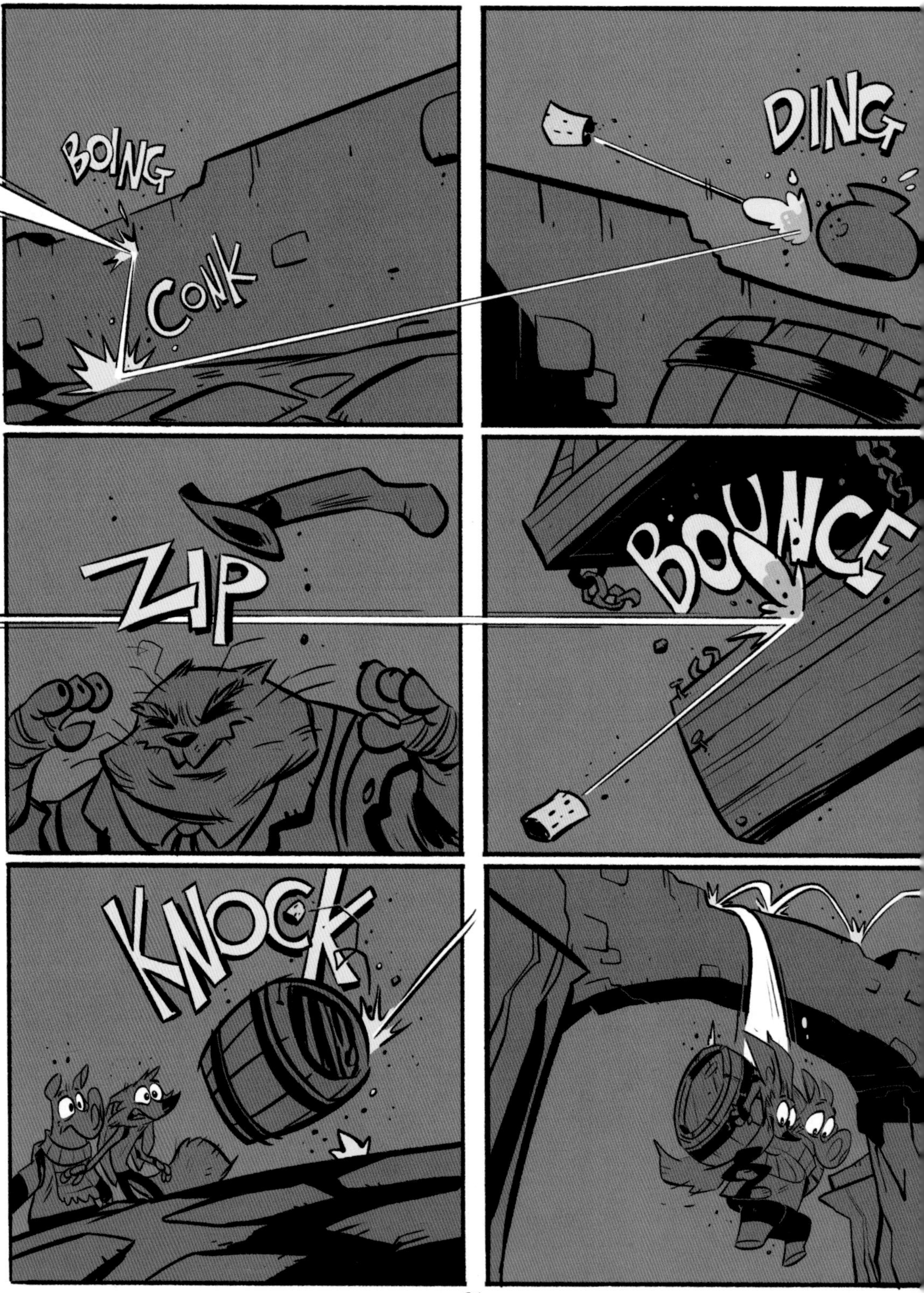
BOING
CONK
DING
ZIP
BOUNCE
KNOCK

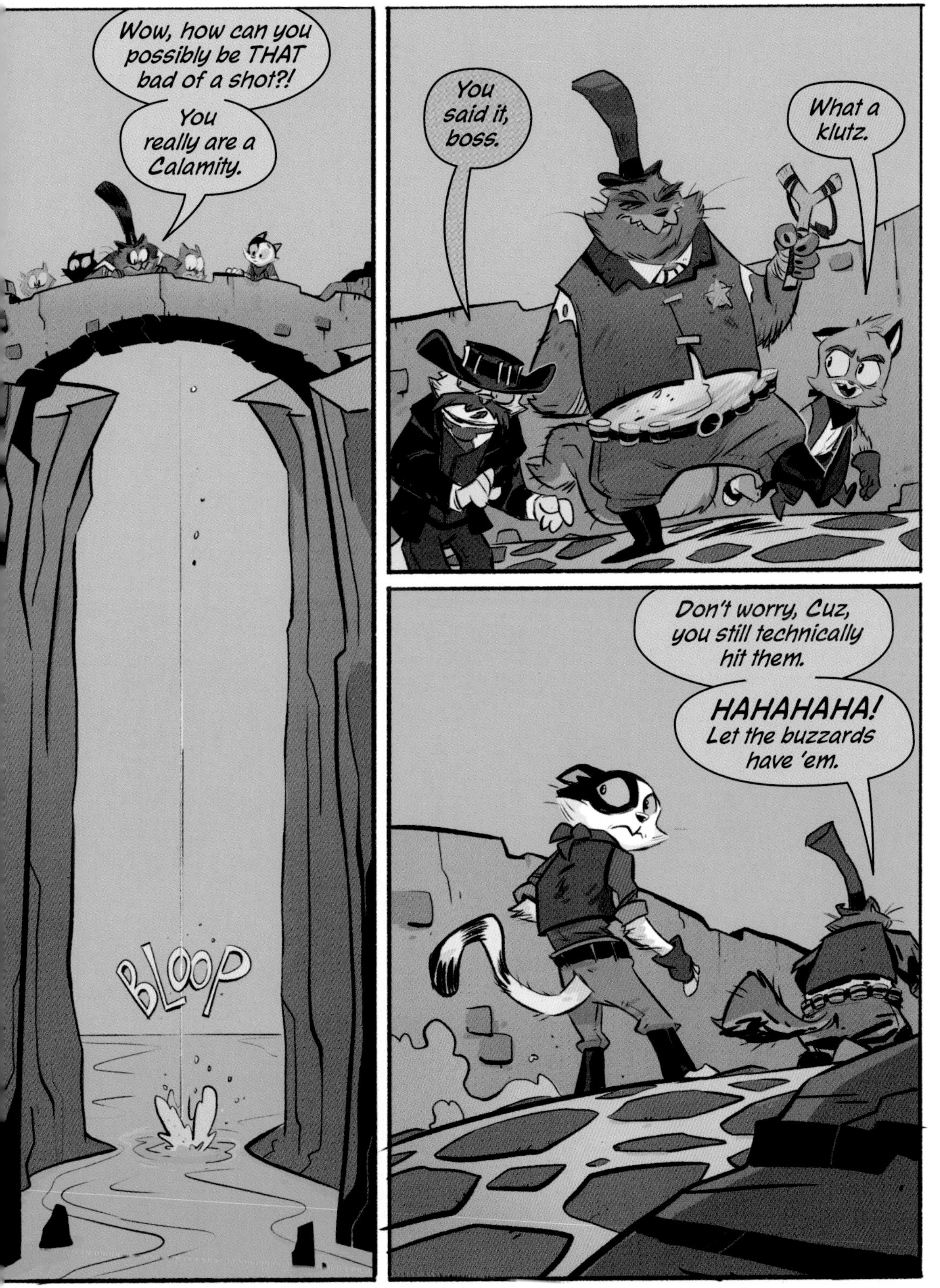
Wow, how can you possibly be THAT bad of a shot?!
You really are a Calamity.
BLOOP
You said it, boss.
What a klutz.
Don't worry, Cuz, you still technically hit them.
HAHAHAHA! Let the buzzards have 'em.

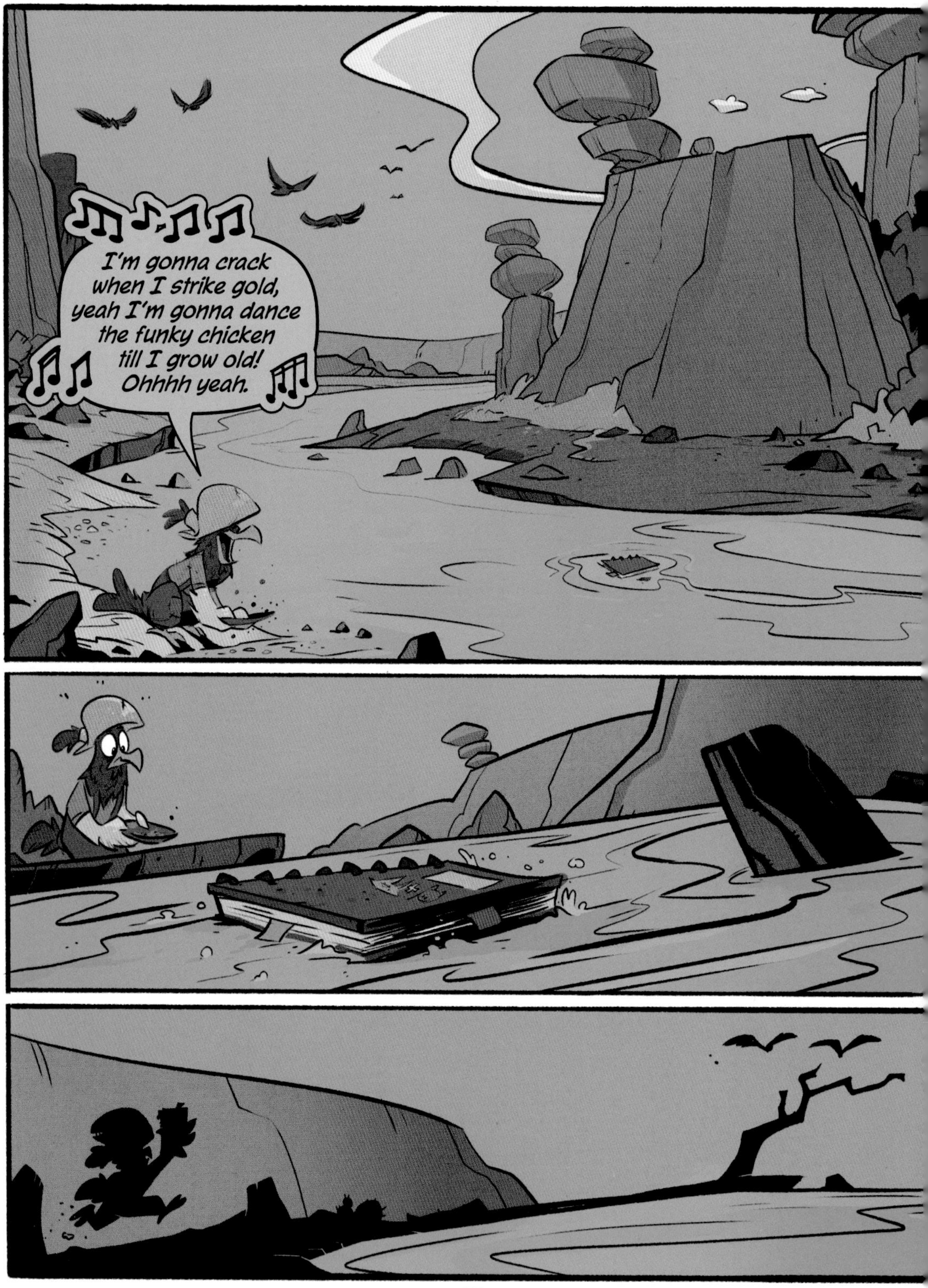
I'm gonna crack when I strike gold, yeah I'm gonna dance the funky chicken till I grow old! Ohhhh yeah.

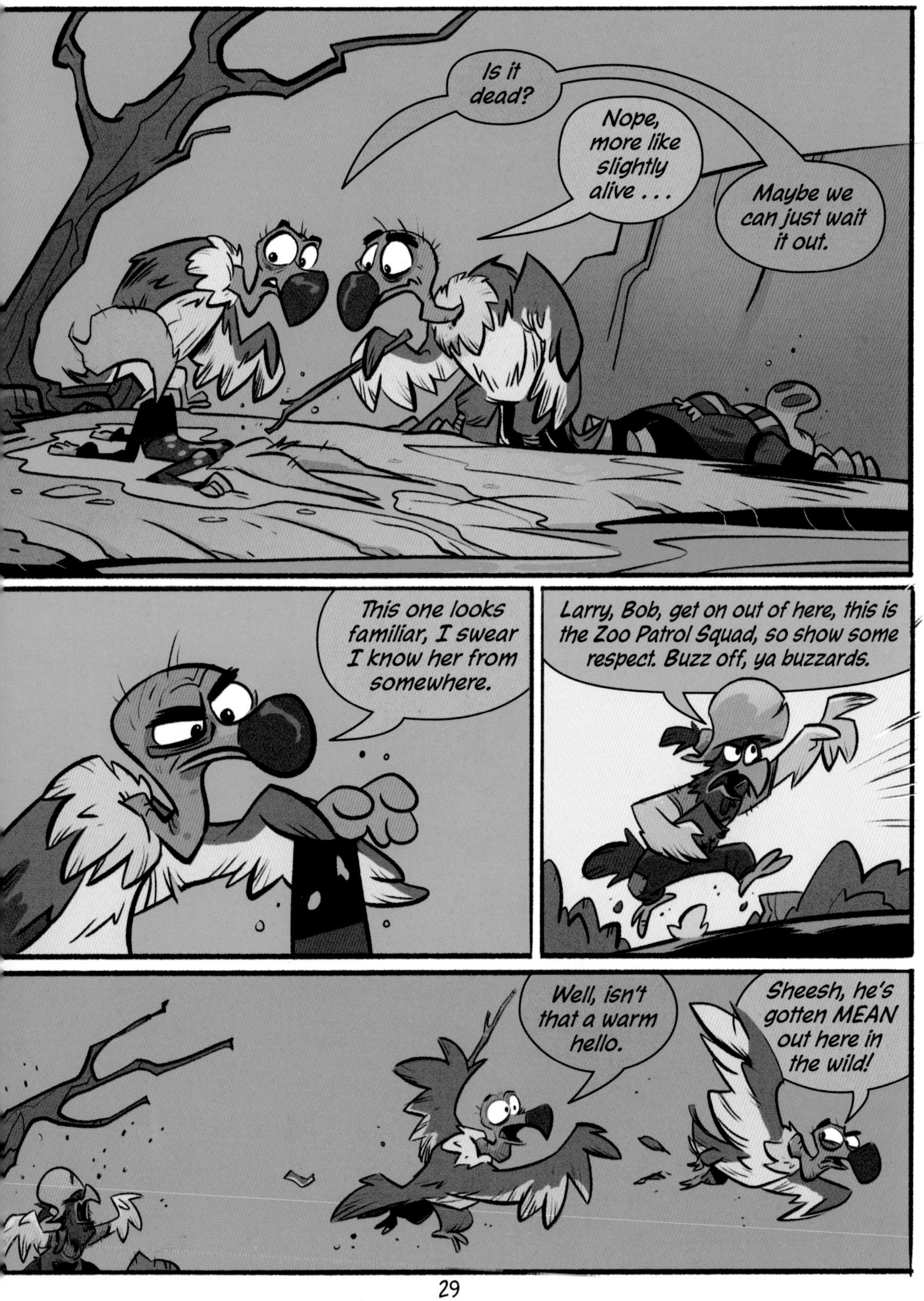
Is it dead?
Nope, more like slightly alive . . .
Maybe we can just wait it out.
This one looks familiar, I swear I know her from somewhere.
Larry, Bob, get on out of here, this is the Zoo Patrol Squad, so show some respect. Buzz off, ya buzzards.
Well, isn't that a warm hello.
Sheesh, he's gotten MEAN out here in the wild!

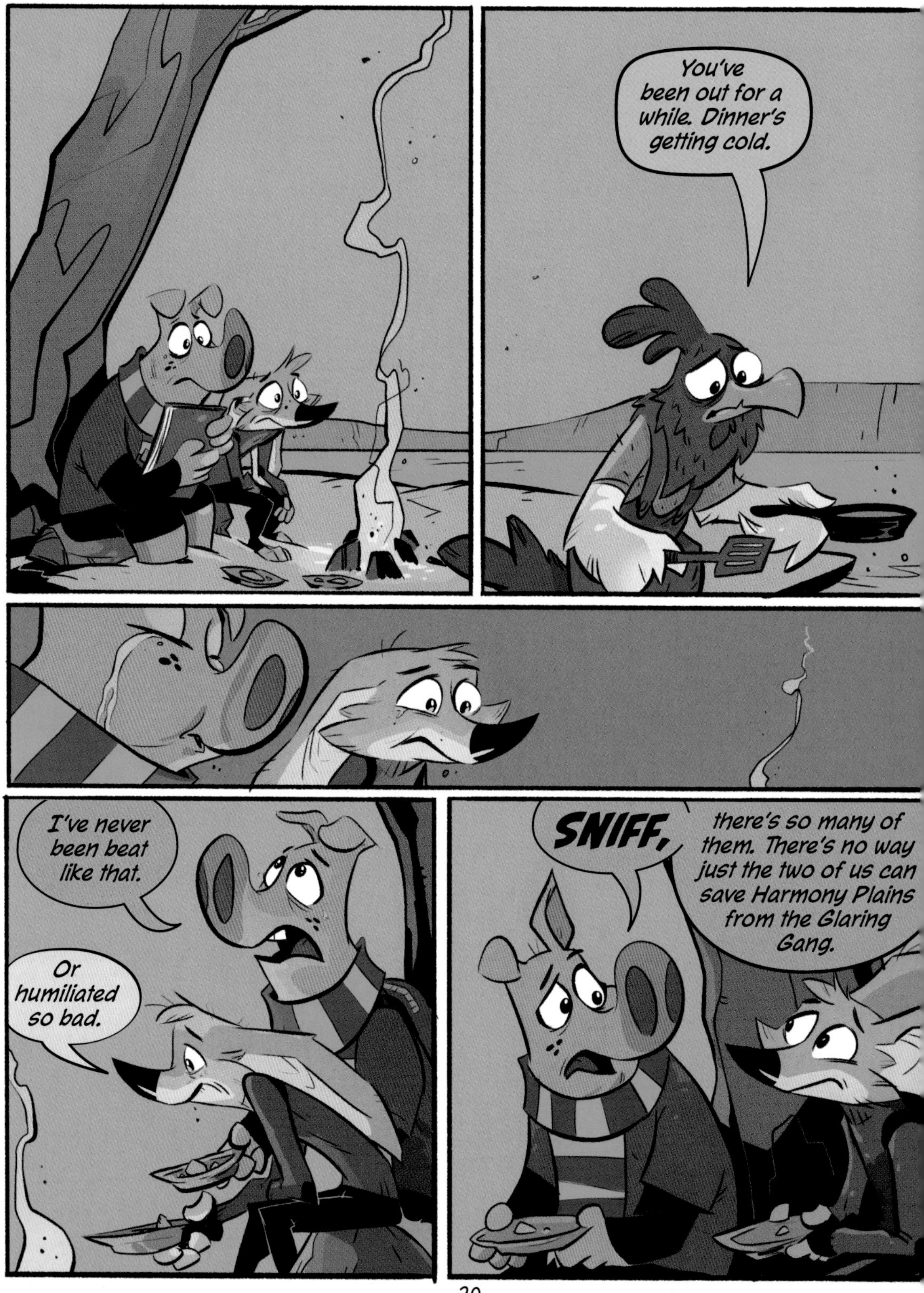
You've been out for a while. Dinner's getting cold.
I've never been beat like that.
Or humiliated so bad.
SNIFF,
there's so many of them. There's no way just the two of us can save Harmony Plains from the Glaring Gang.

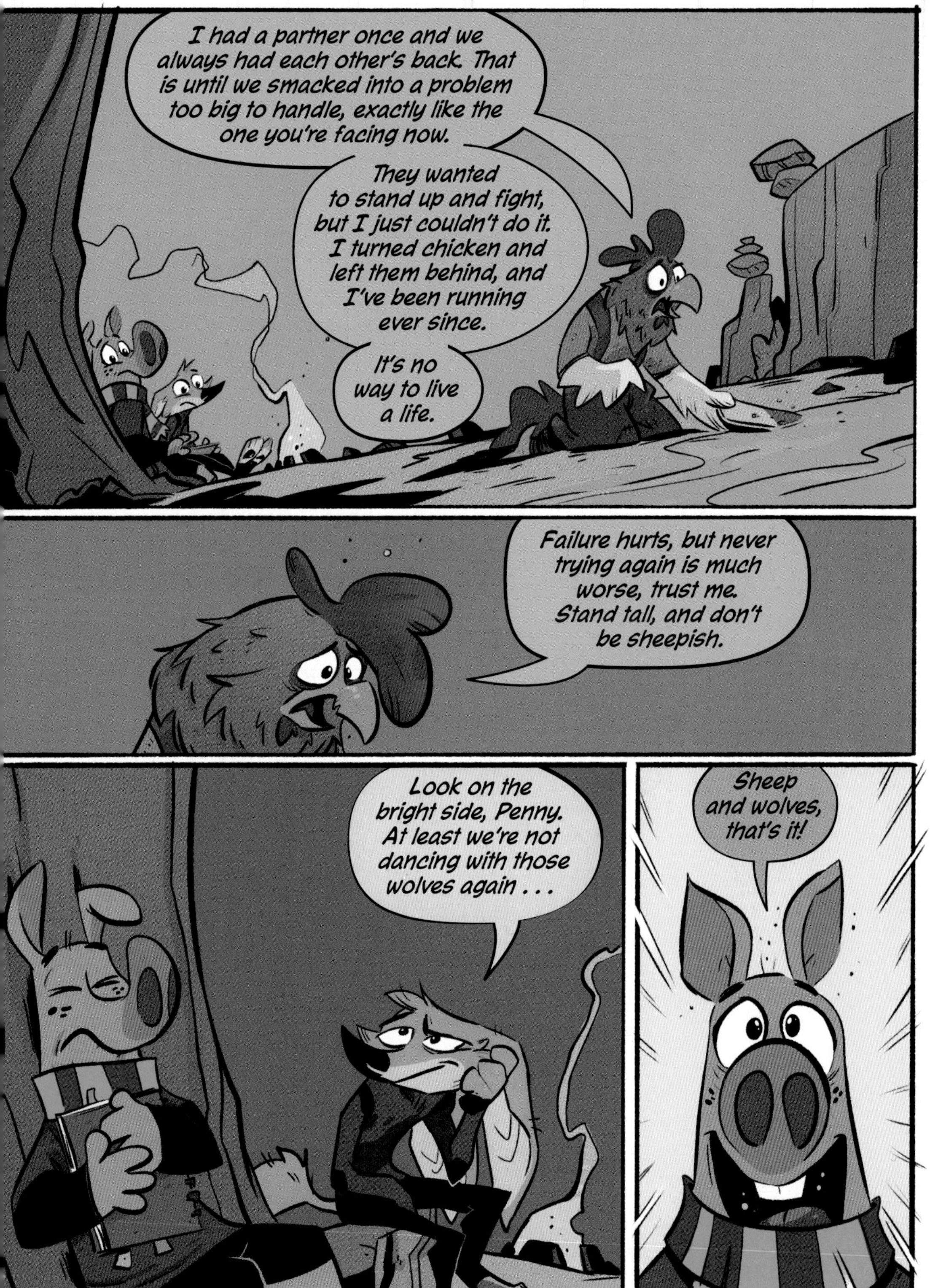
I had a partner once and we always had each other's back. That is until we smacked into a problem too big to handle, exactly like the one you're facing now.
They wanted to stand up and fight, but I just couldn't do it. I turned chicken and left them behind, and I've been running ever since.
It's no way to live a life.
Failure hurts, but never trying again is much worse, trust me. Stand tall, and don't be sheepish.
Look on the bright side, Penny. At least we're not dancing with those wolves again . . .
Sheep and wolves, that's it!

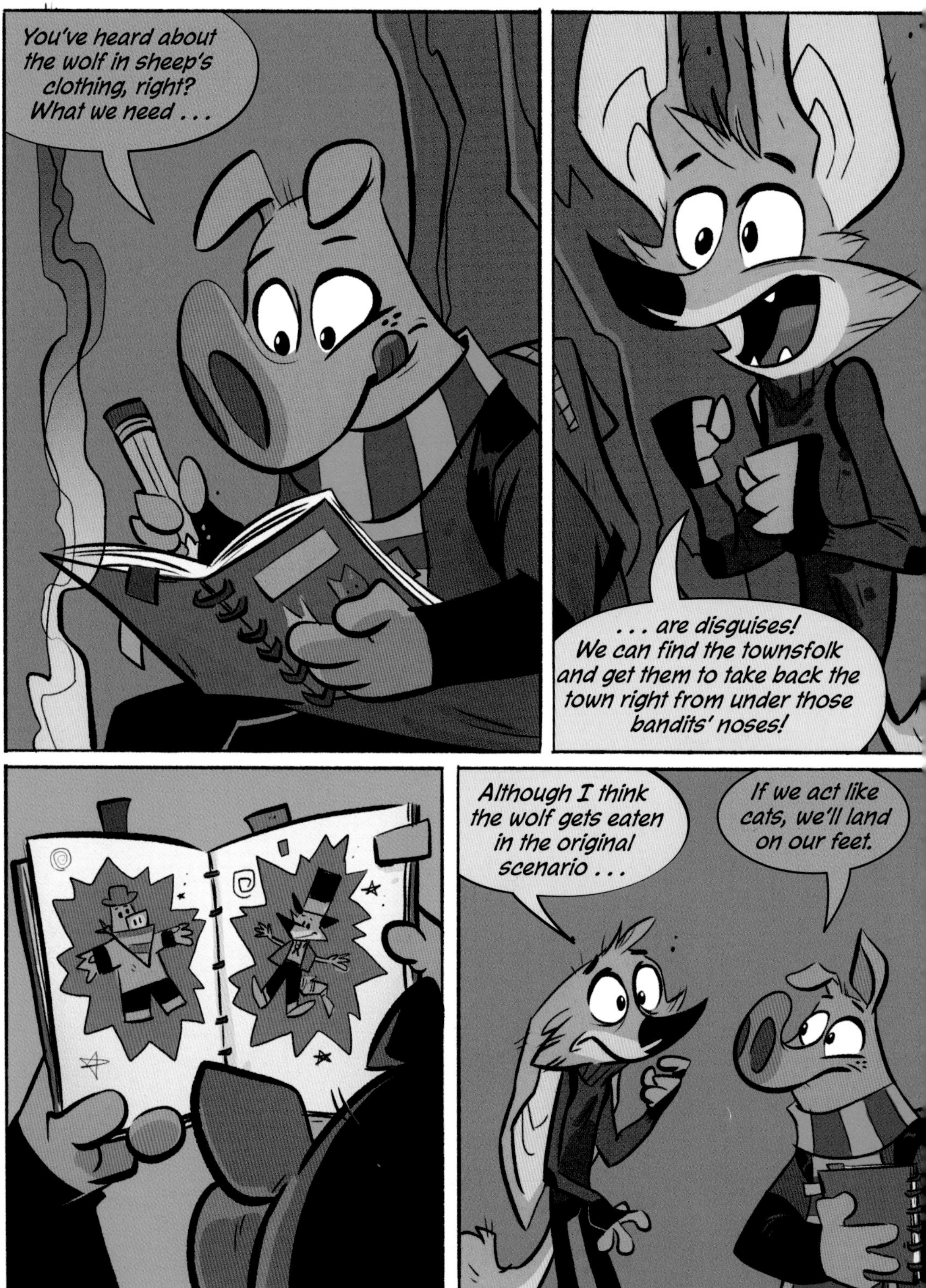
You've heard about the wolf in sheep's clothing, right? What we need . . .
. . . are disguises! We can find the townsfolk and get them to take back the town right from under those bandits' noses!
Although I think the wolf gets eaten in the original scenario . . .
If we act like cats, we'll land on our feet.

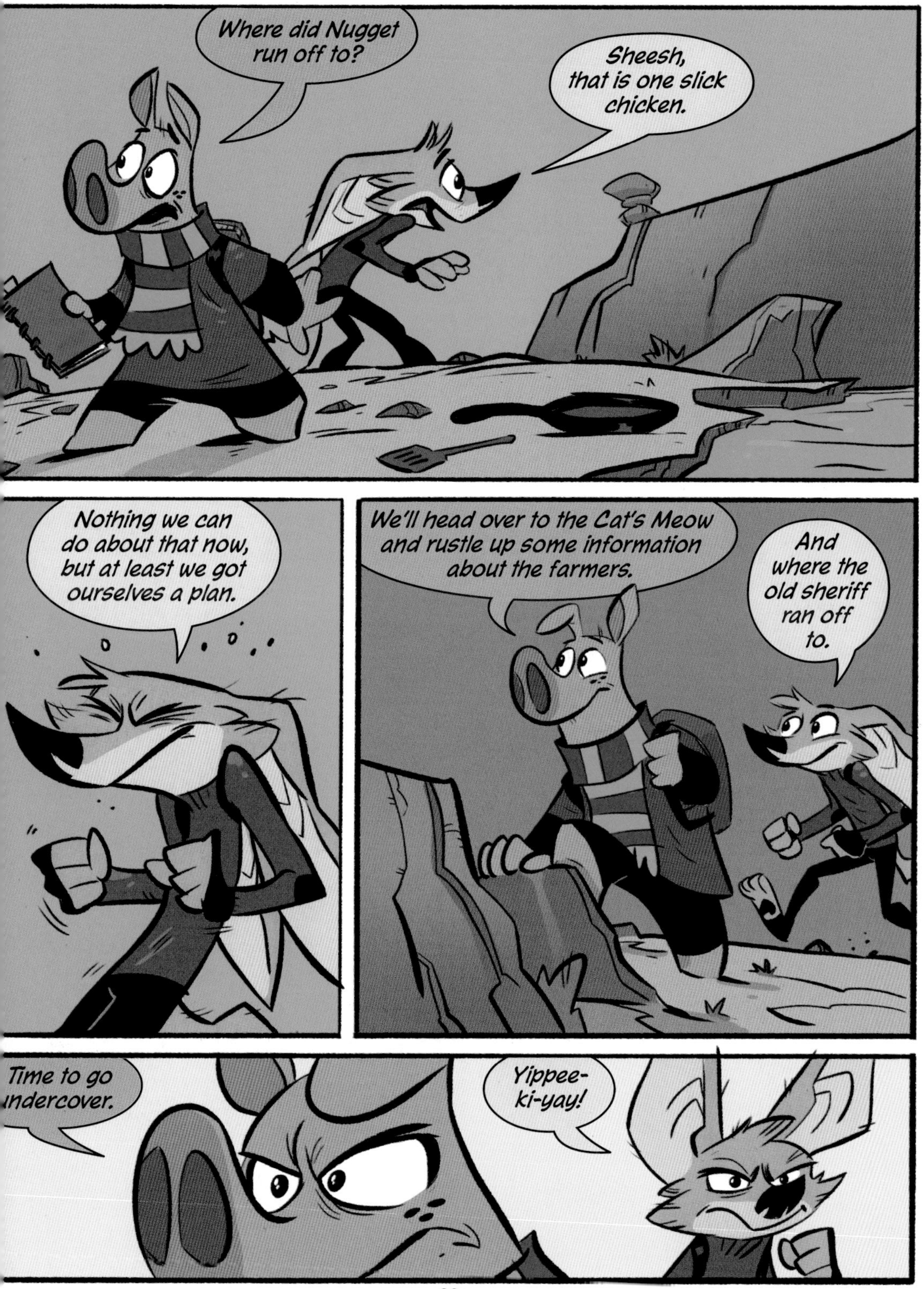

Where did Nugget run off to?
Sheesh, that is one slick chicken.
Nothing we can do about that now, but at least we got ourselves a plan.
We'll head over to the Cat's Meow and rustle up some information about the farmers.
And where the old sheriff ran off to.
Time to go undercover.
Yippee-ki-yay!

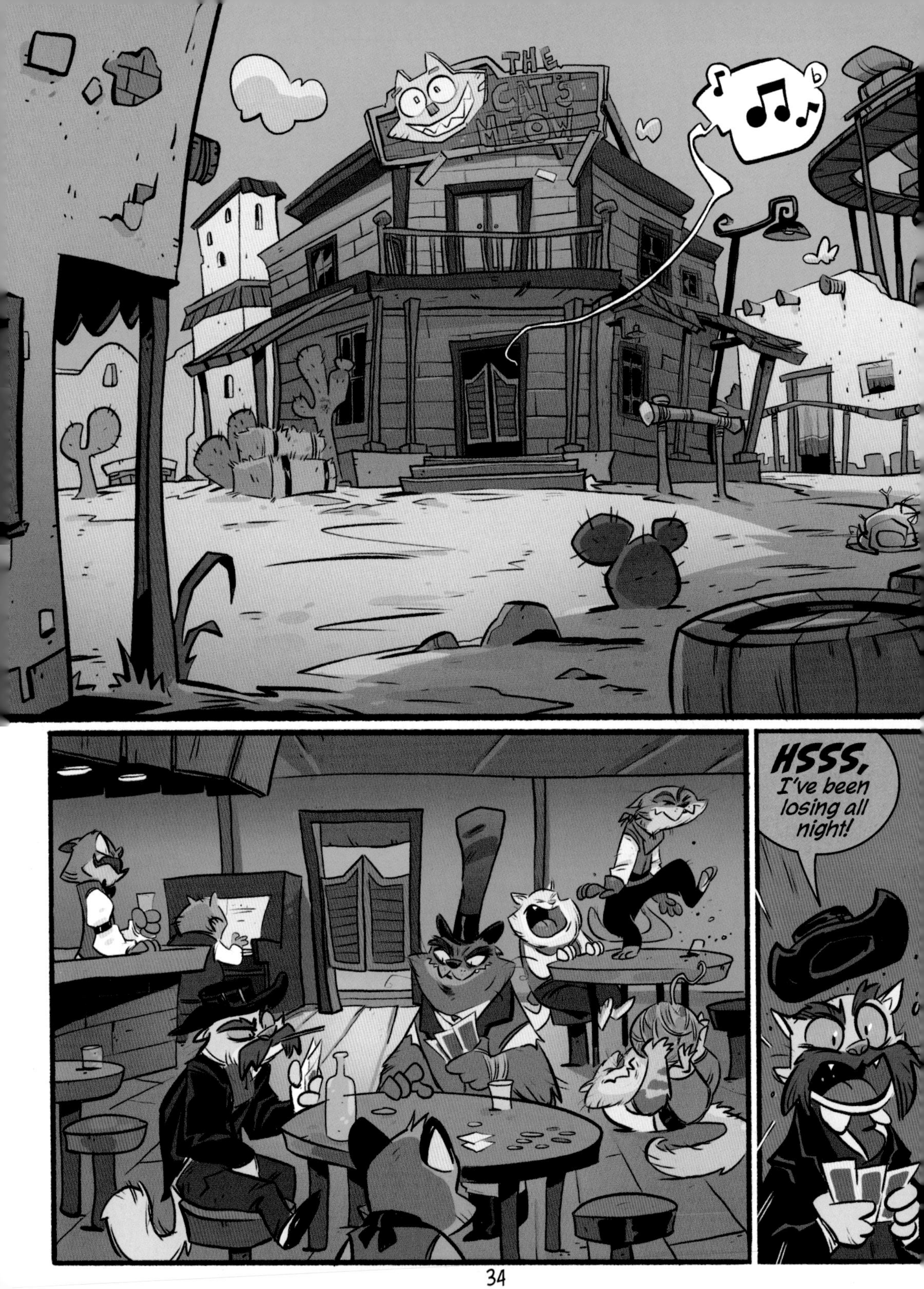
THE CAT'S MEOW!
HSSS, I've been losing all night!

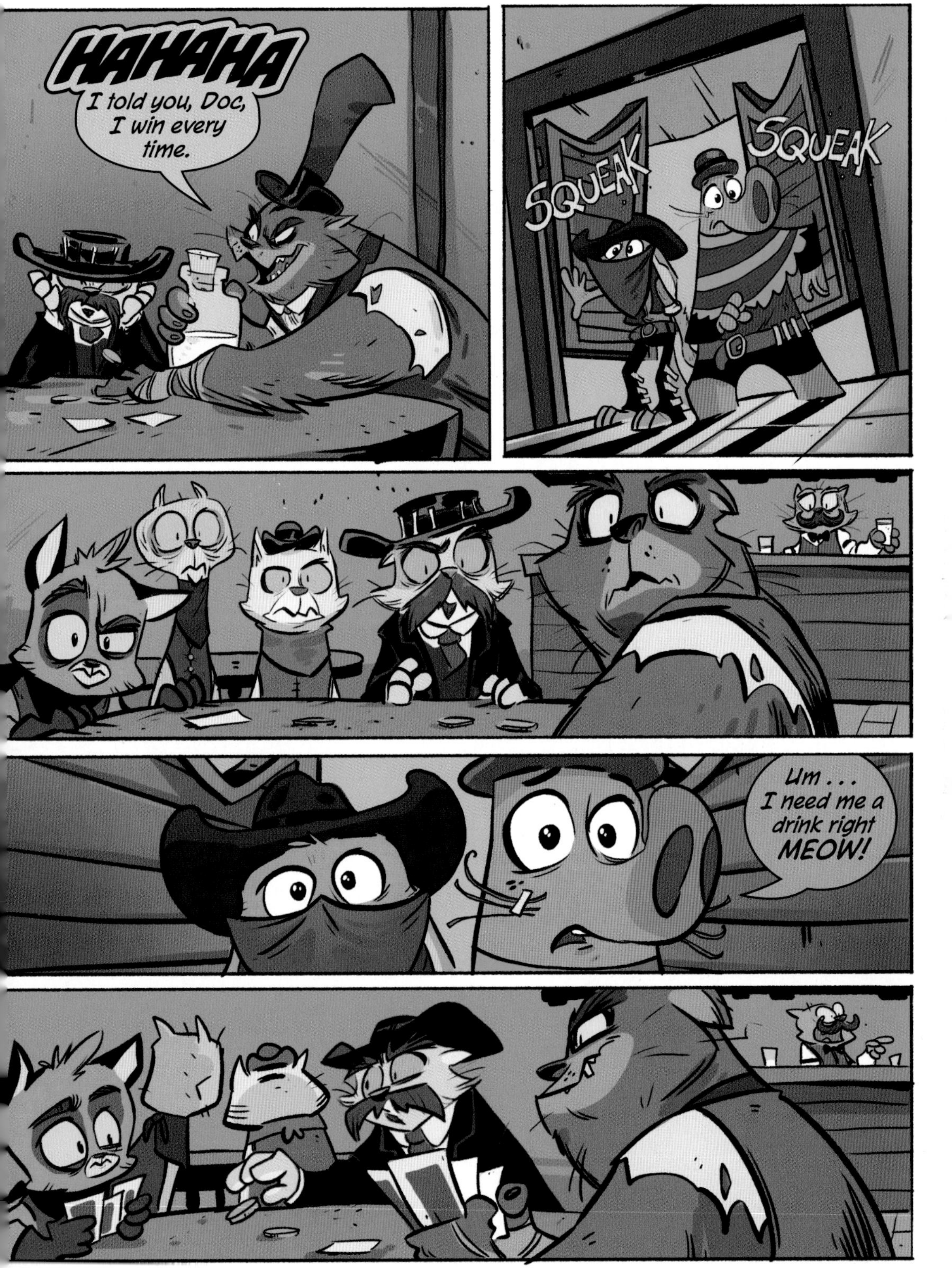
HAHAHA
I told you, Doc, I win every time.
SQUEAK
SQUEAK
Um . . . I need me a drink right MEOW!

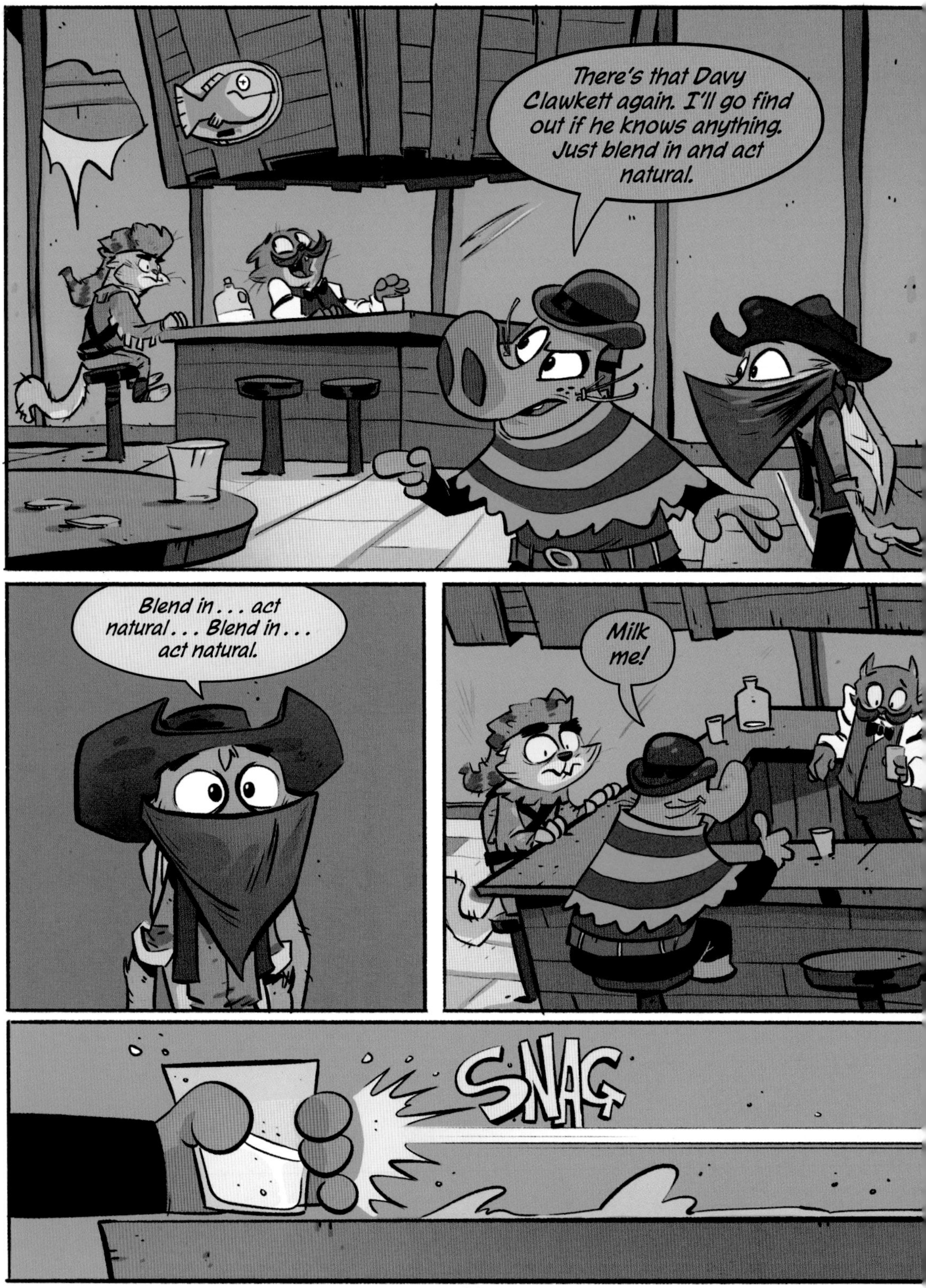

There's that Davy Clawkett again. I'll go find out if he knows anything. Just blend in and act natural.
Blend in . . . act natural . . . Blend in . . . act natural.
Milk me!
SNAG

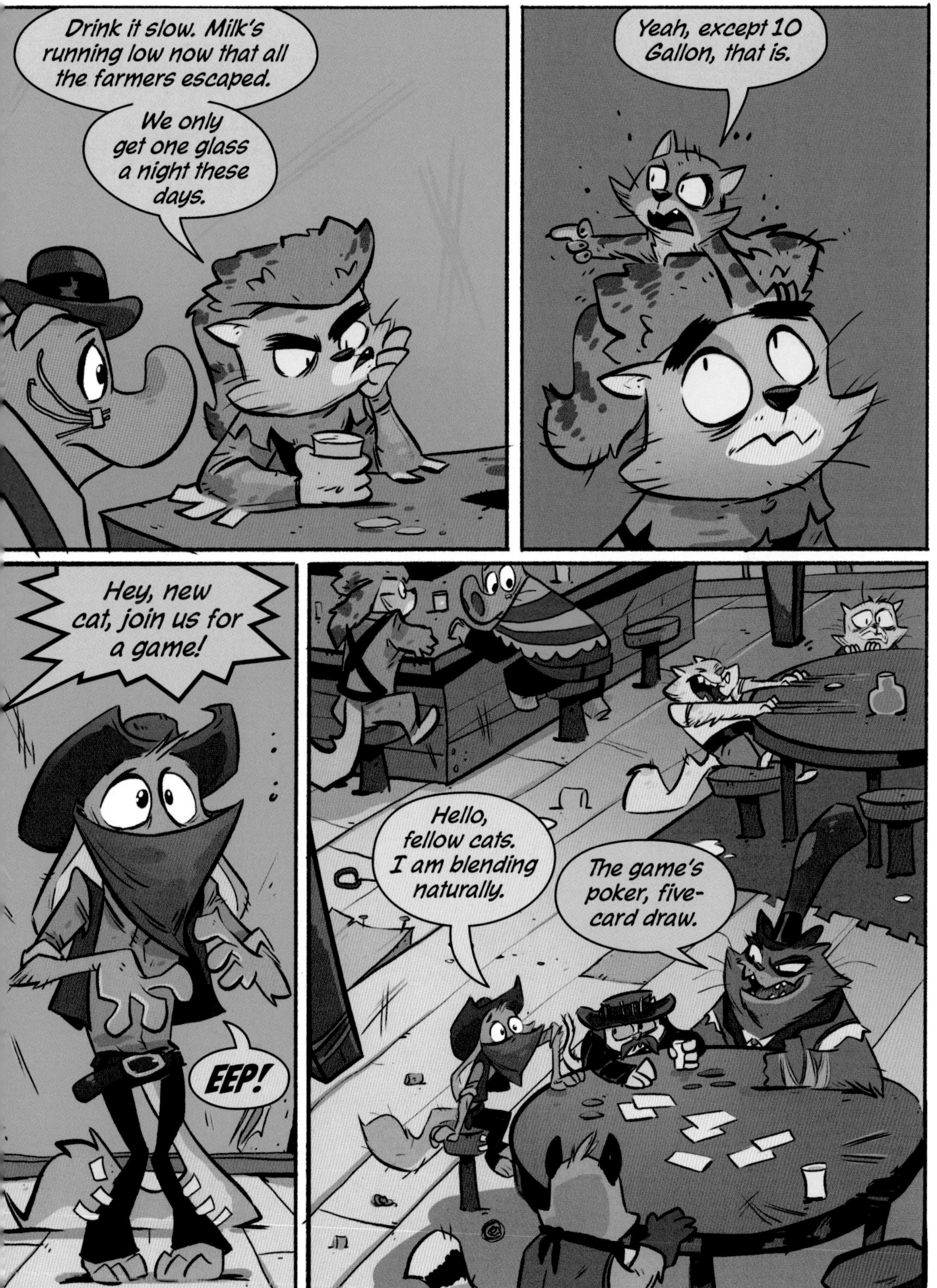
Drink it slow. Milk's running low now that all the farmers escaped.
We only get one glass a night these days.
Yeah, except 10 Gallon, that is.
Hey, new cat, join us for a game!
EEP!
Hello, fellow cats. I am blending naturally.
The game's poker, five-card draw.

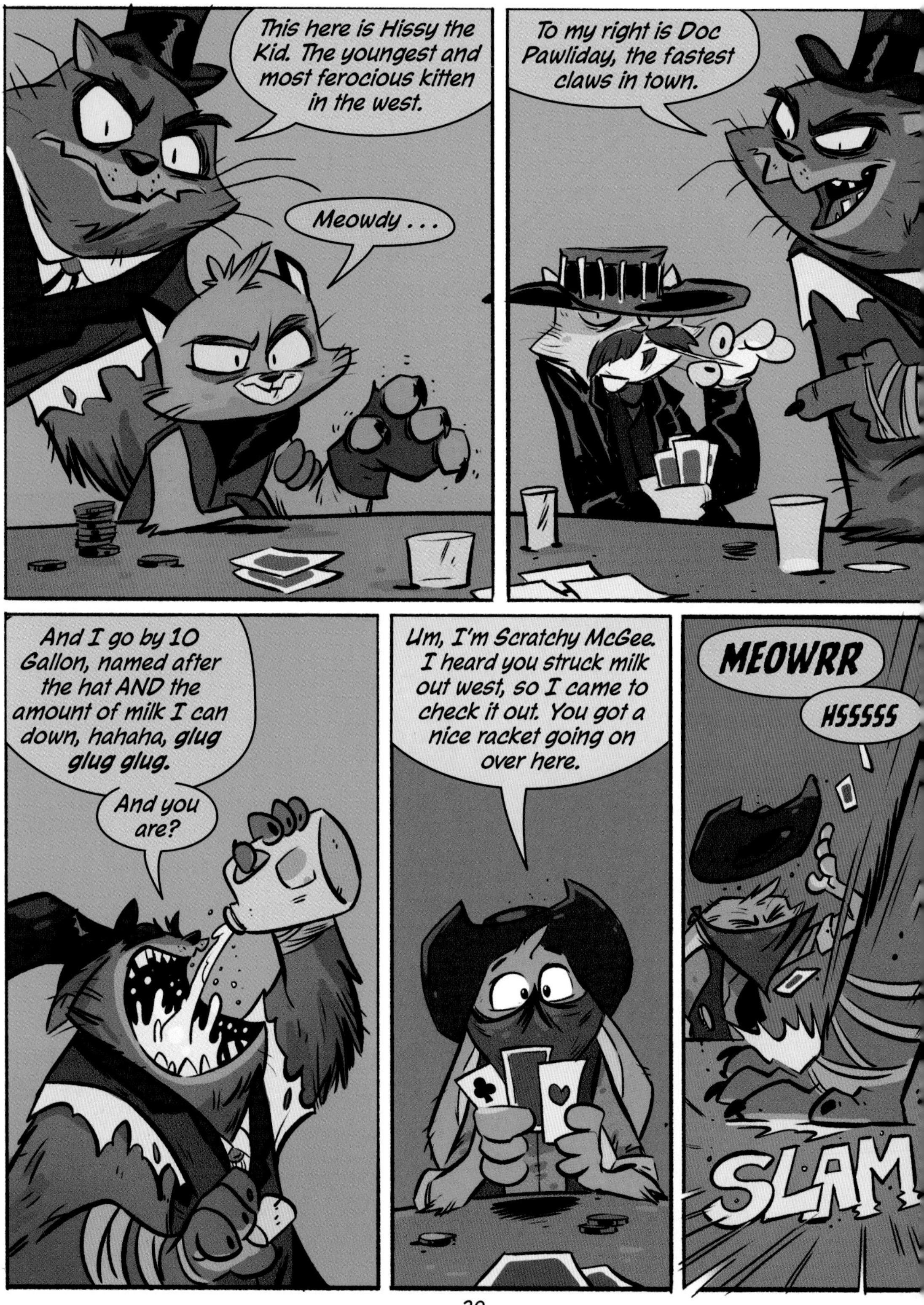
This here is Hissy the Kid. The youngest and most ferocious kitten in the west.
Meowdy . . .
To my right is Doc Pawliday, the fastest claws in town.
And I go by 10 Gallon, named after the hat AND the amount of milk I can down, hahaha, glug glug glug.
And you are?
Um, I'm Scratchy McGee. I heard you struck milk out west, so I came to check it out. You got a nice racket going on over here.
MEOWRR
HSSSSS
SLAM

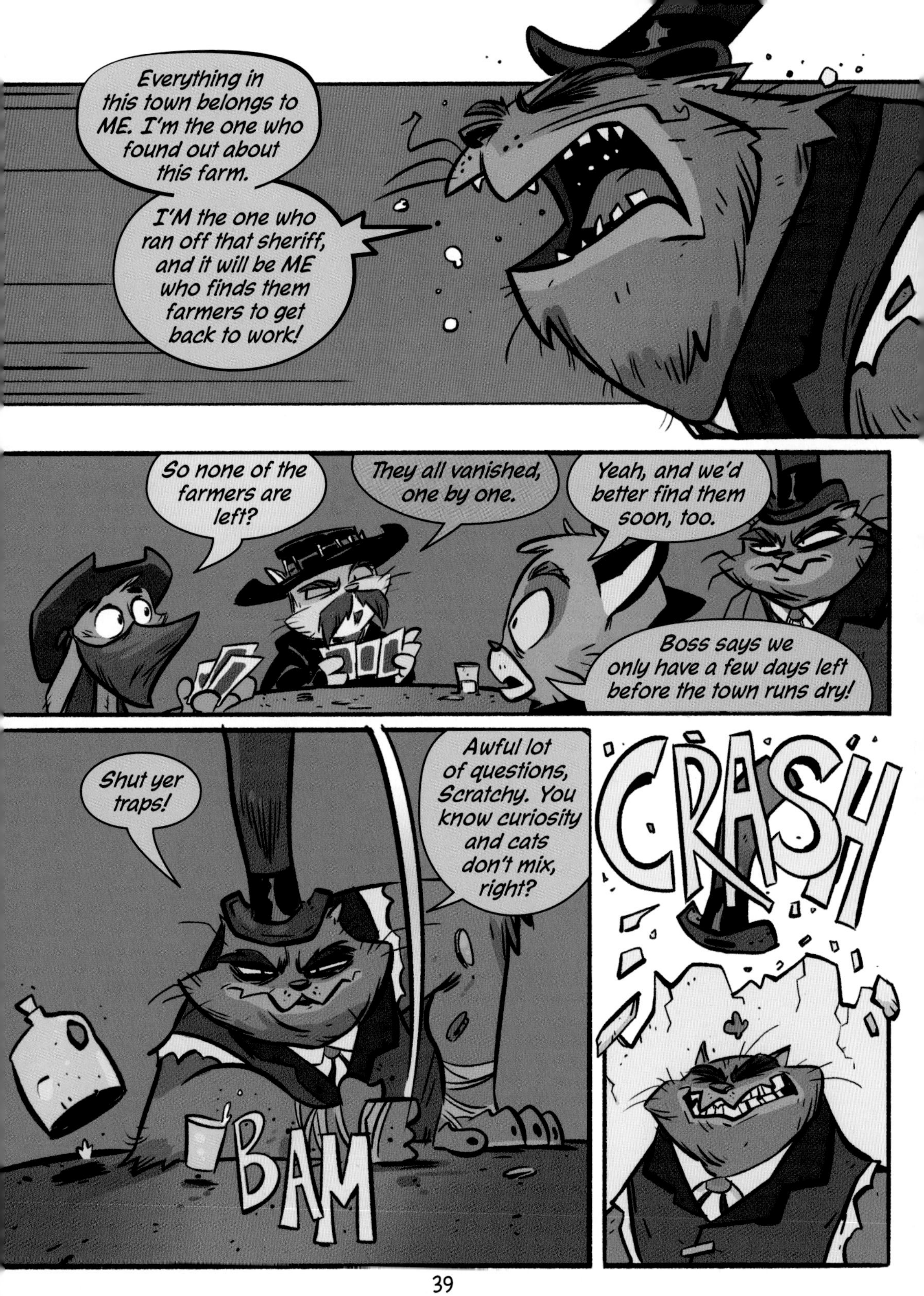
Everything in this town belongs to ME. I'm the one who found out about this farm.
I'M the one who ran off that sheriff, and it will be ME who finds them farmers to get back to work!
So none of the farmers are left?
They all vanished, one by one.
Yeah, and we'd better find them soon, too.
Boss says we only have a few days left before the town runs dry!
Shut yer traps!
Awful lot of questions, Scratchy. You know curiosity and cats don't mix, right?
BAM
CRASH

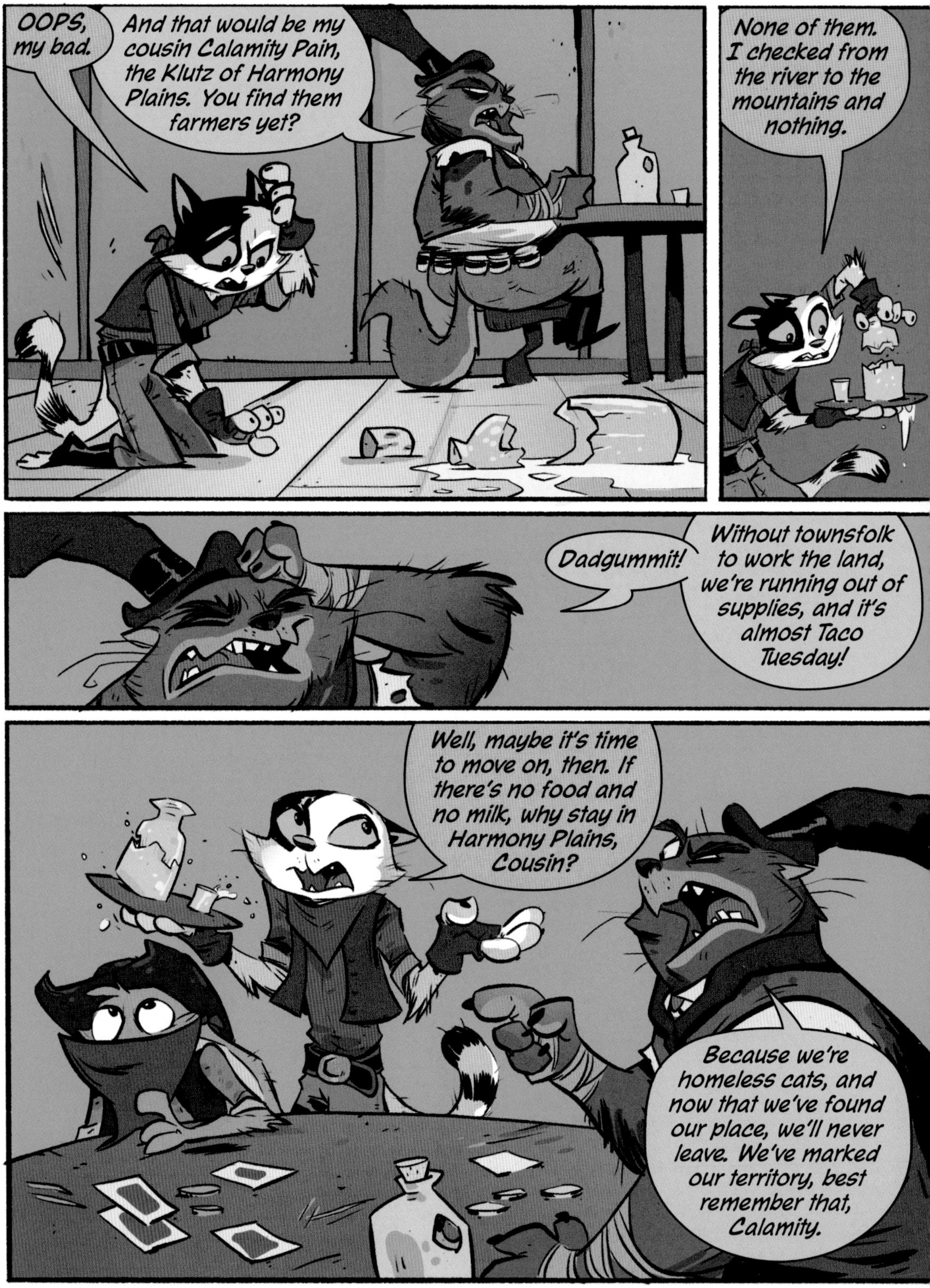
OOPS, my bad.
And that would be my cousin Calamity Pain, the Klutz of Harmony Plains. You find them farmers yet?
None of them. I checked from the river to the mountains and nothing.
Dadgummit!
Without townsfolk to work the land, we're running out of supplies, and it's almost Taco Tuesday!
Well, maybe it's time to move on, then. If there's no food and no milk, why stay in Harmony Plains, Cousin?
Because we're homeless cats, and now that we've found our place, we'll never leave. We've marked our territory, best remember that, Calamity.

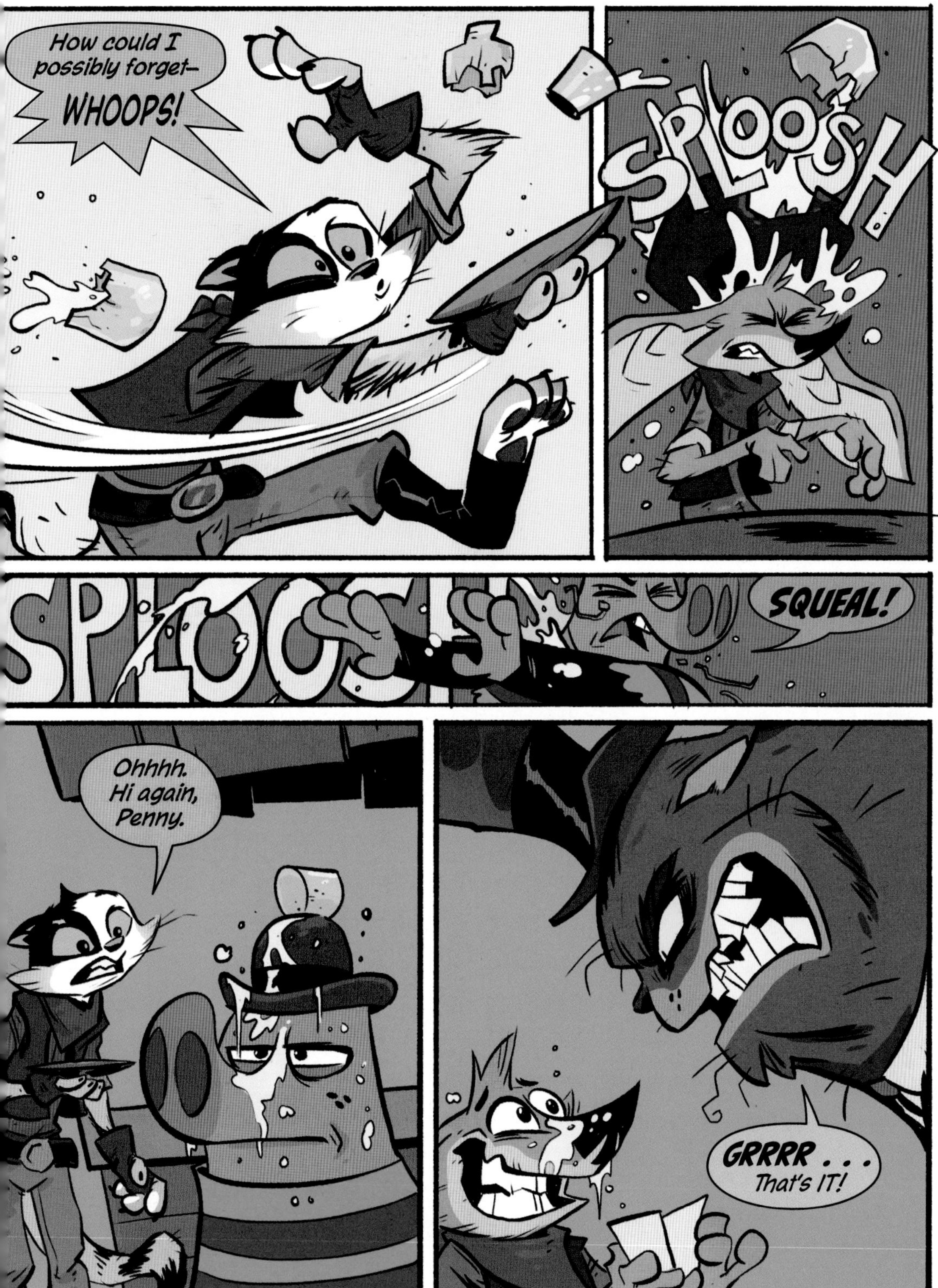
How could I possibly forget—
WHOOPS!
SPLOOSH!
SPLOOSH
SQUEAL!
Ohhhh. Hi again, Penny.
GRRRR . . . That's IT!

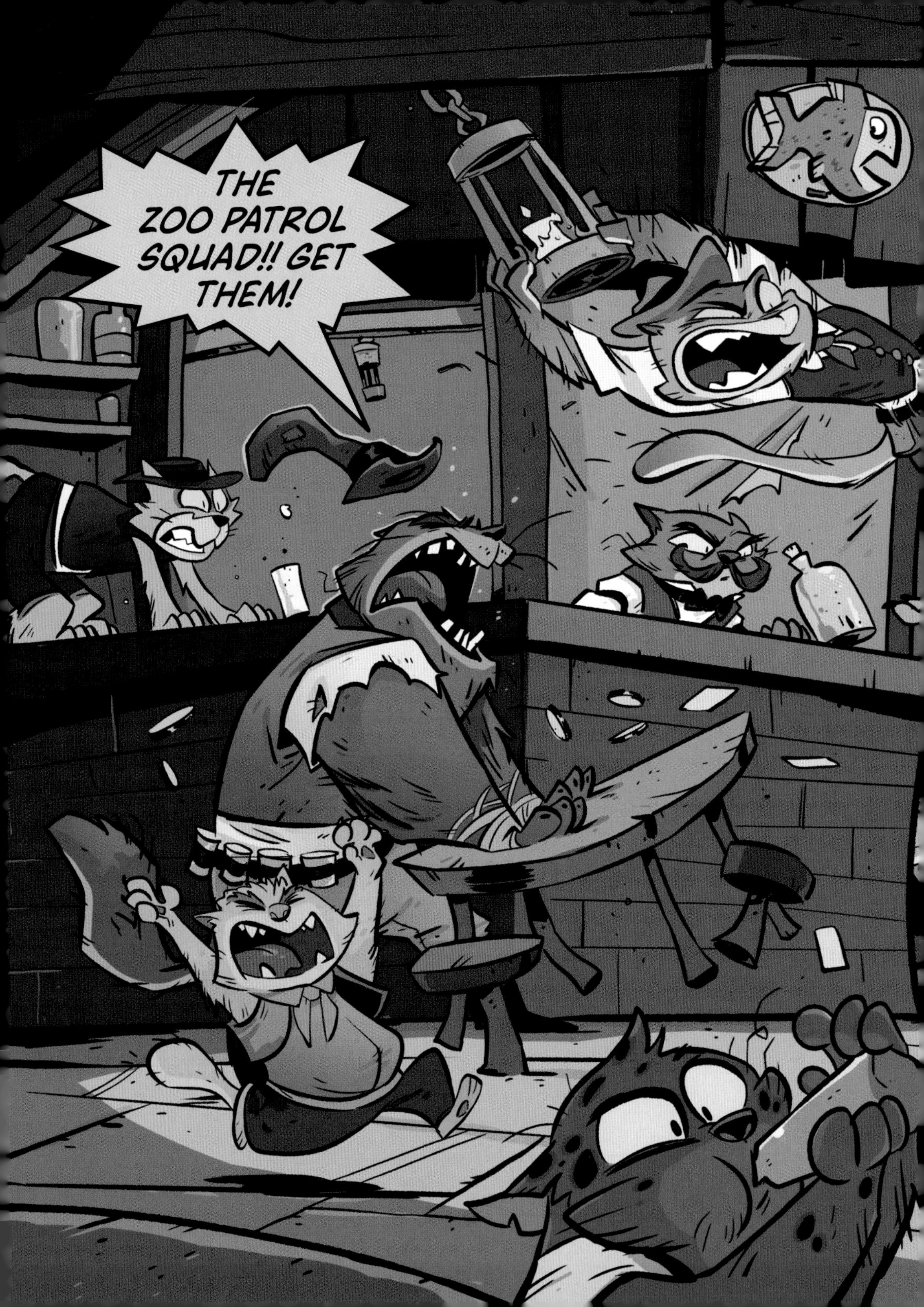
THE ZOO PATROL SQUAD!! GET THEM!

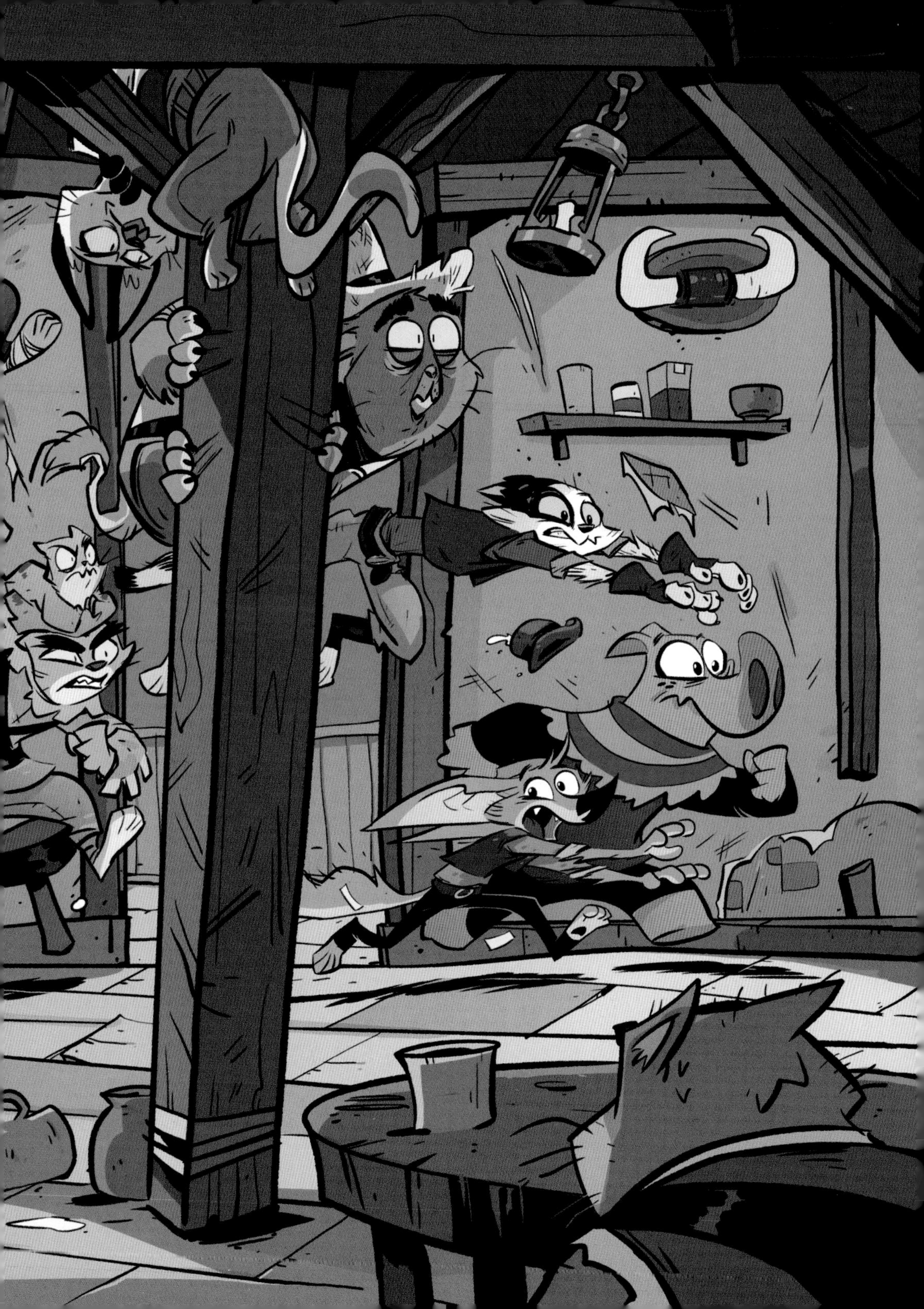

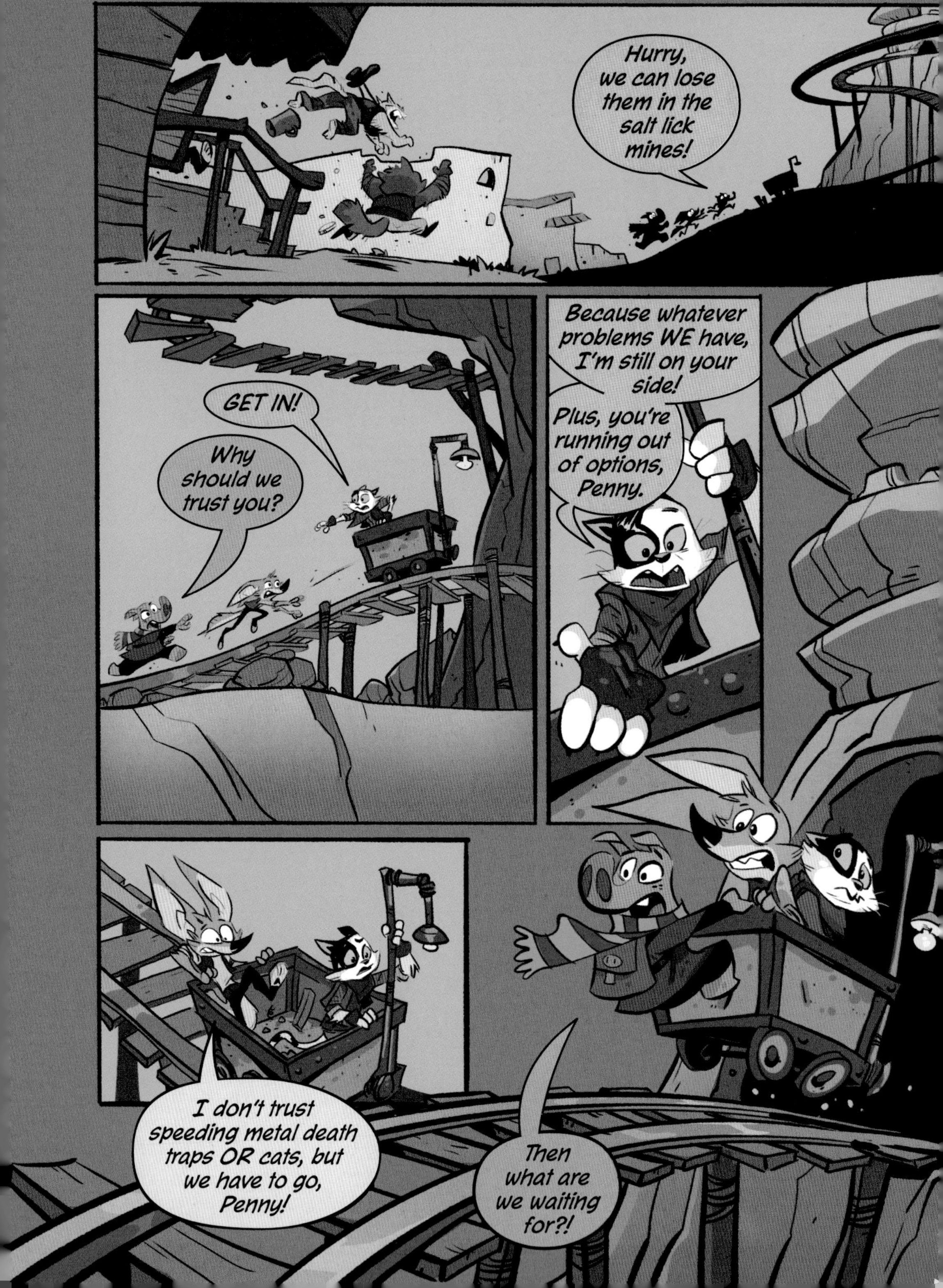
Hurry, we can lose them in the salt lick mines!
GET IN!
Why should we trust you?
Because whatever problems WE have, I'm still on your side!
Plus, you're running out of options, Penny.
I don't trust speeding metal death traps OR cats, but we have to go, Penny!
Then what are we waiting for?!

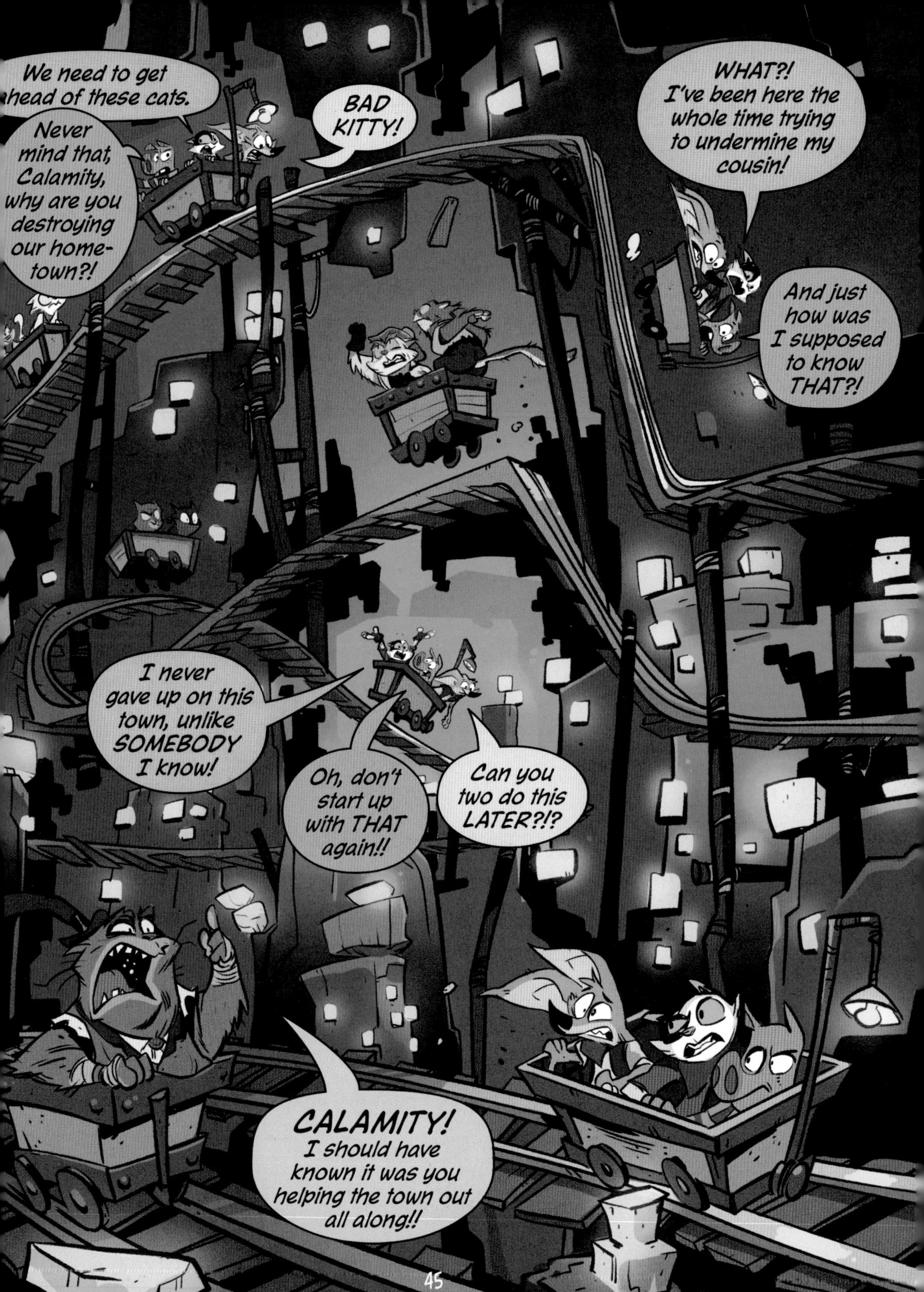
We need to get ahead of these cats.
Never mind that, Calamity, why are you destroying our hometown?!
BAD KITTY!
WHAT?! I've been here the whole time trying to undermine my cousin!
And just how was I supposed to know THAT?!
I never gave up on this town, unlike SOMEBODY I know!
Oh, don't start up with THAT again!!
Can you two do this LATER?!?
CALAMITY! I should have known it was you helping the town out all along!!

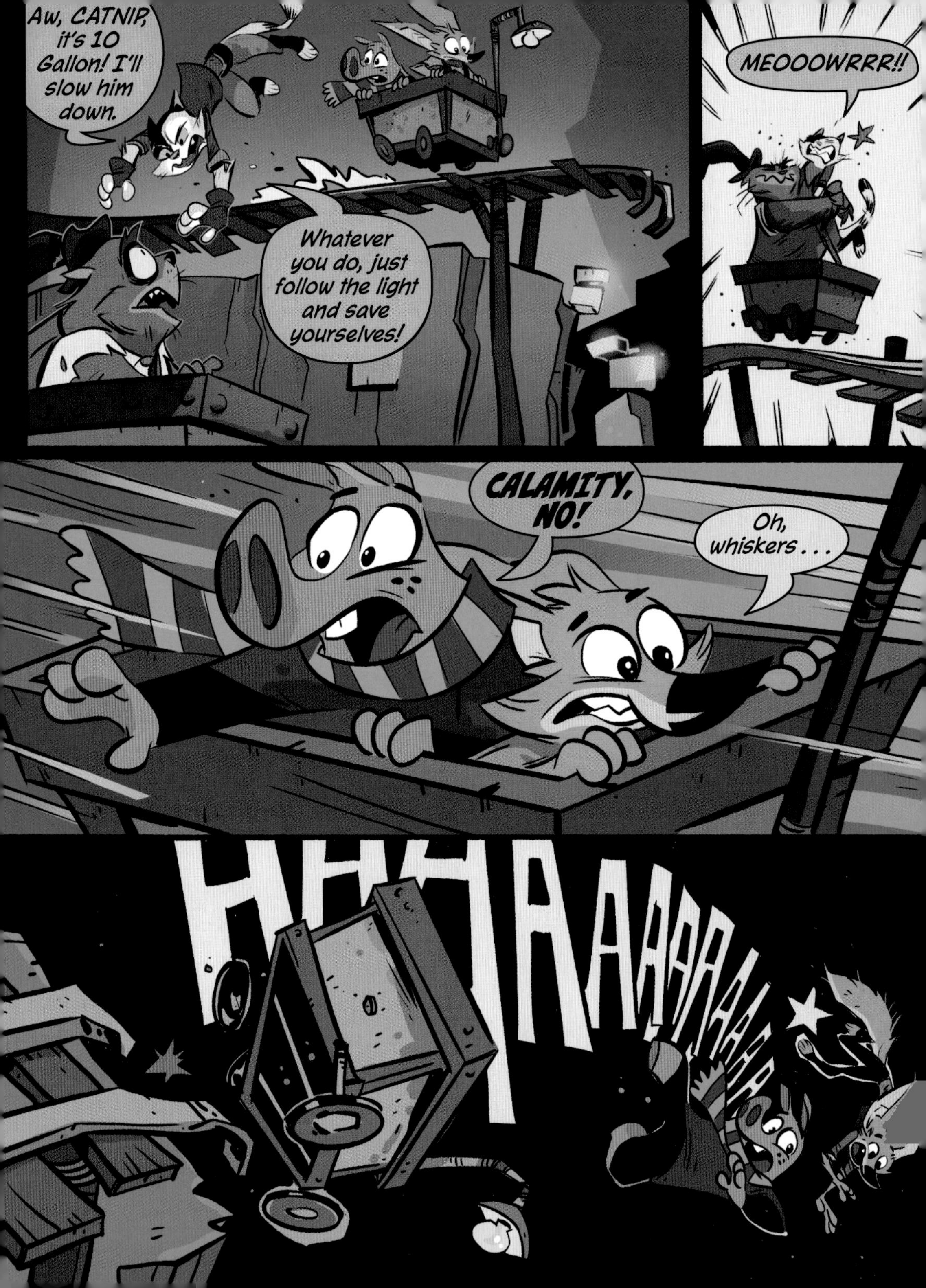

Aw, CATNIP, it's 10 Gallon! I'll slow him down.
Whatever you do, just follow the light and save yourselves!
MEOOOWRRR!!
CALAMITY, NO!
Oh, whiskers . . .

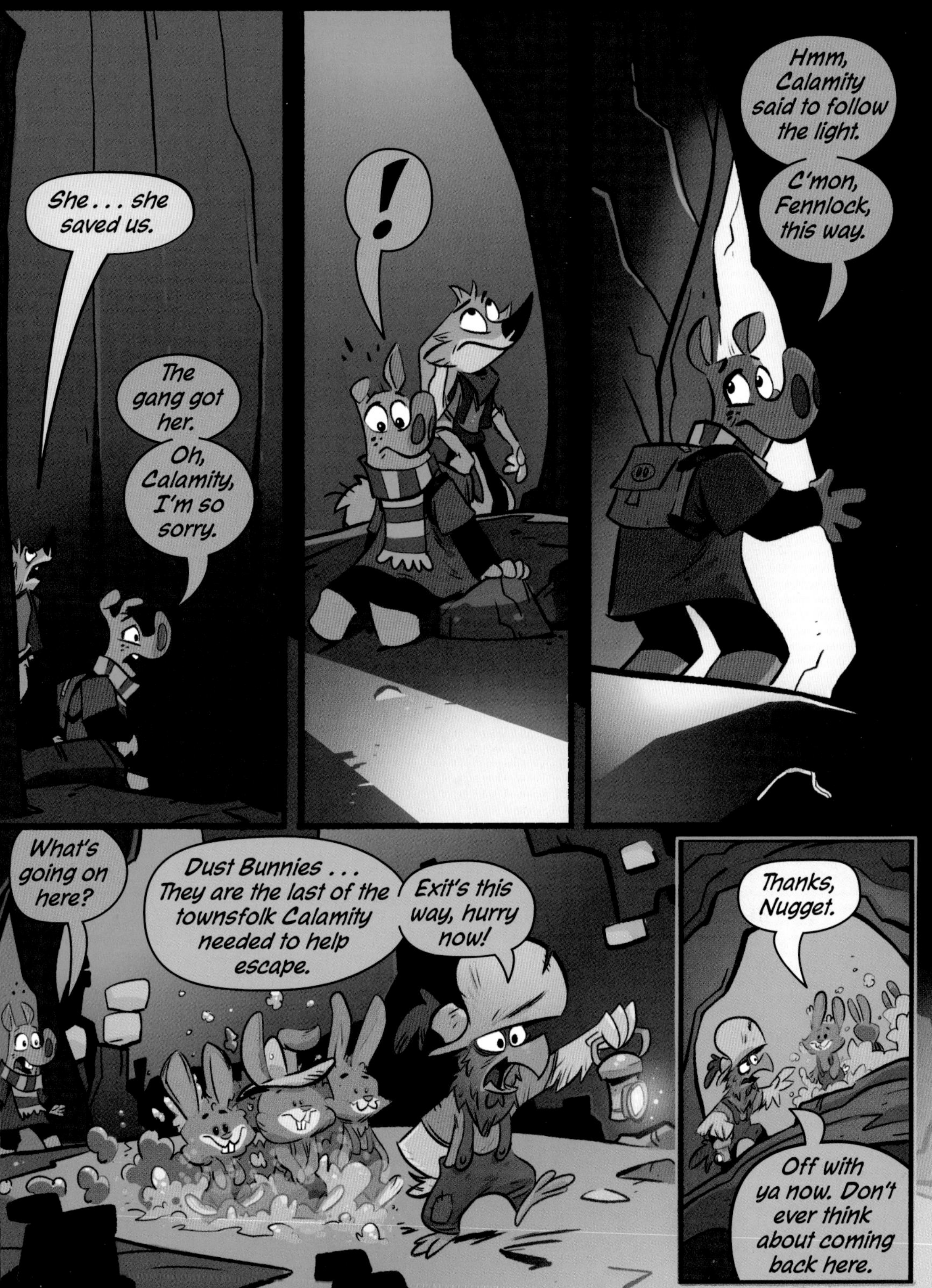
She . . . she saved us.
The gang got her.
Oh, Calamity, I'm so sorry.
!
Hmm, Calamity said to follow the light.
C'mon, Fennlock, this way.
What's going on here?
Dust Bunnies . . . They are the last of the townsfolk Calamity needed to help escape.
Exit's this way, hurry now!
Thanks, Nugget.
Off with ya now. Don't ever think about coming back here.

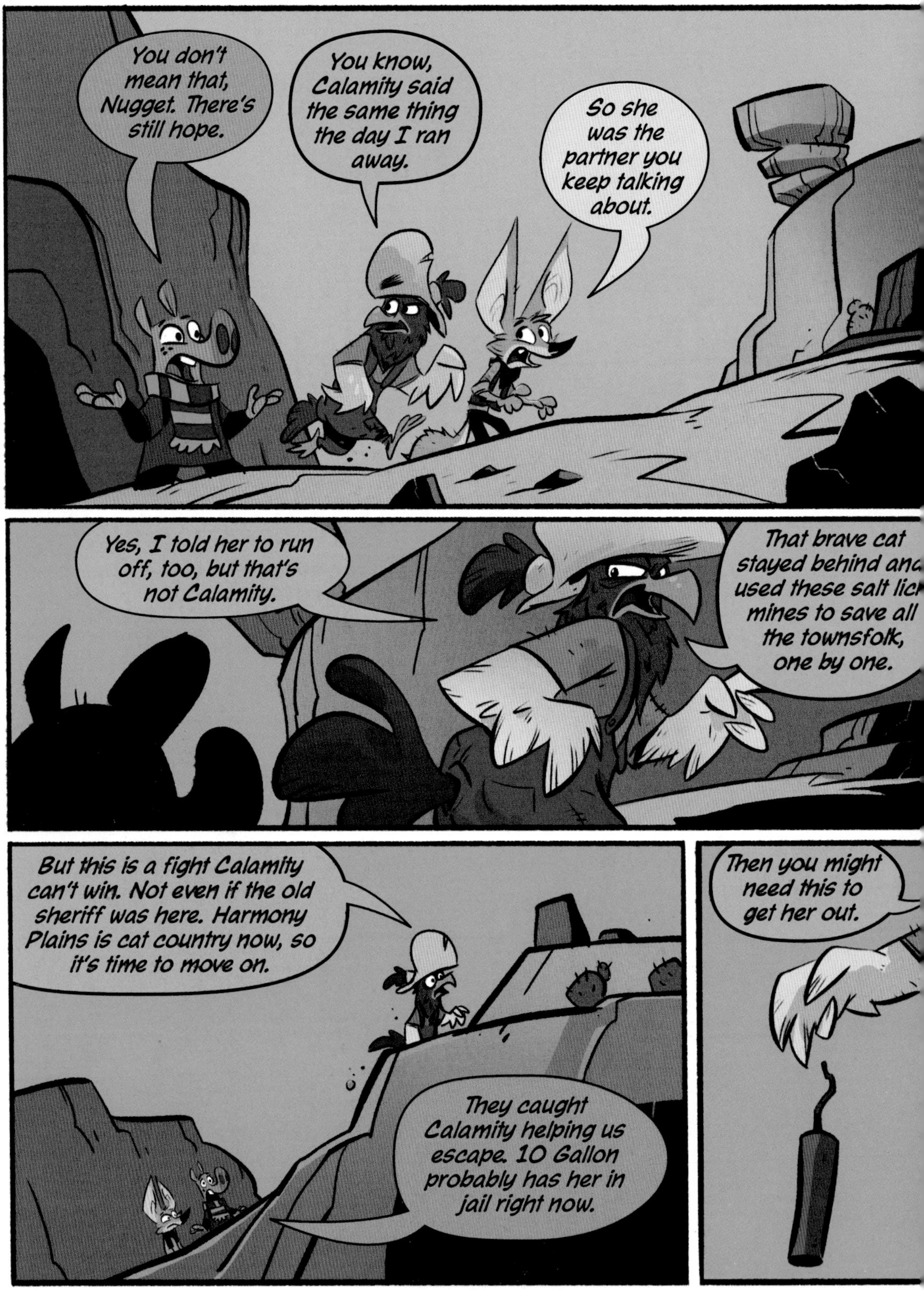
You don't mean that, Nugget. There's still hope.
You know, Calamity said the same thing the day I ran away.
So she was the partner you keep talking about.
Yes, I told her to run off, too, but that's not Calamity.
That brave cat stayed behind and used these salt lick mines to save all the townsfolk, one by one.
But this is a fight Calamity can't win. Not even if the old sheriff was here. Harmony Plains is cat country now, so it's time to move on.
They caught Calamity helping us escape. 10 Gallon probably has her in jail right now.
Then you might need this to get her out.

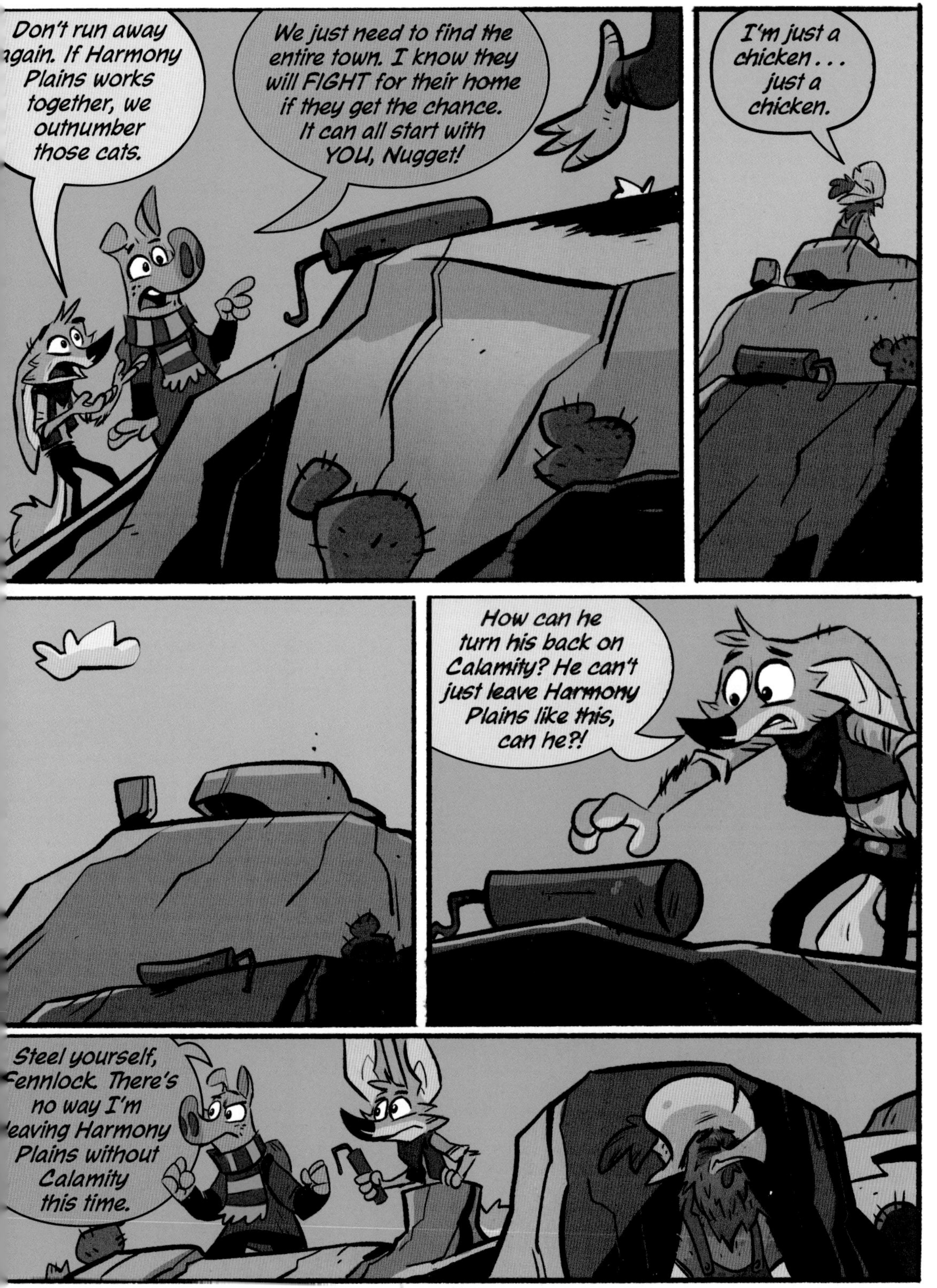
Don't run away again. If Harmony Plains works together, we outnumber those cats.
We just need to find the entire town. I know they will FIGHT for their home if they get the chance. It can all start with YOU, Nugget!
I'm just a chicken . . . just a chicken.
How can he turn his back on Calamity? He can't just leave Harmony Plains like this, can he?!
Steel yourself, Fennlock. There's no way I'm leaving Harmony Plains without Calamity this time.

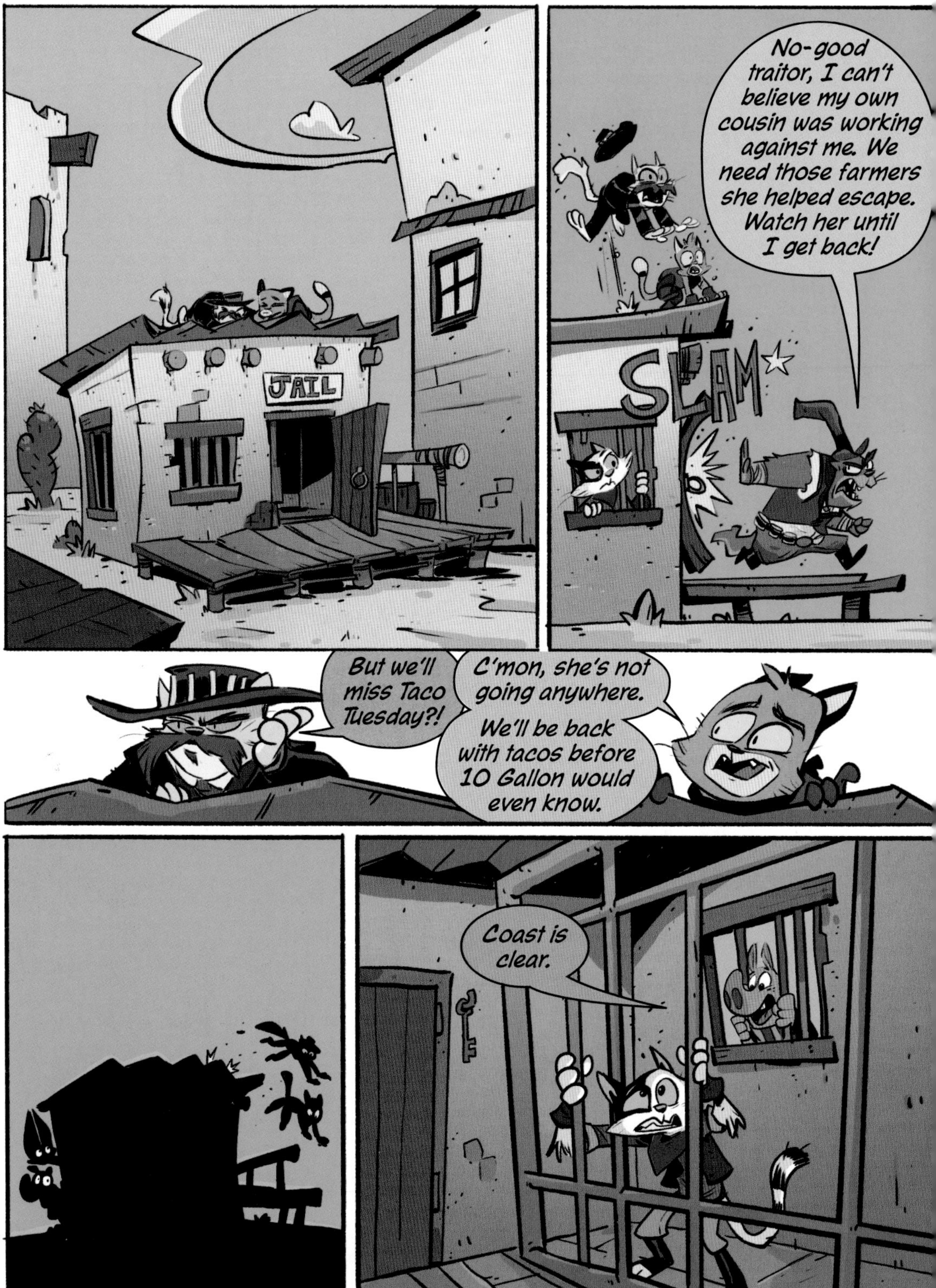
JAIL
No-good traitor, I can't believe my own cousin was working against me. We need those farmers she helped escape. Watch her until I get back!
SLAM
But we'll miss Taco Tuesday?!
C'mon, she's not going anywhere.
We'll be back with tacos before 10 Gallon would even know.
Coast is clear.

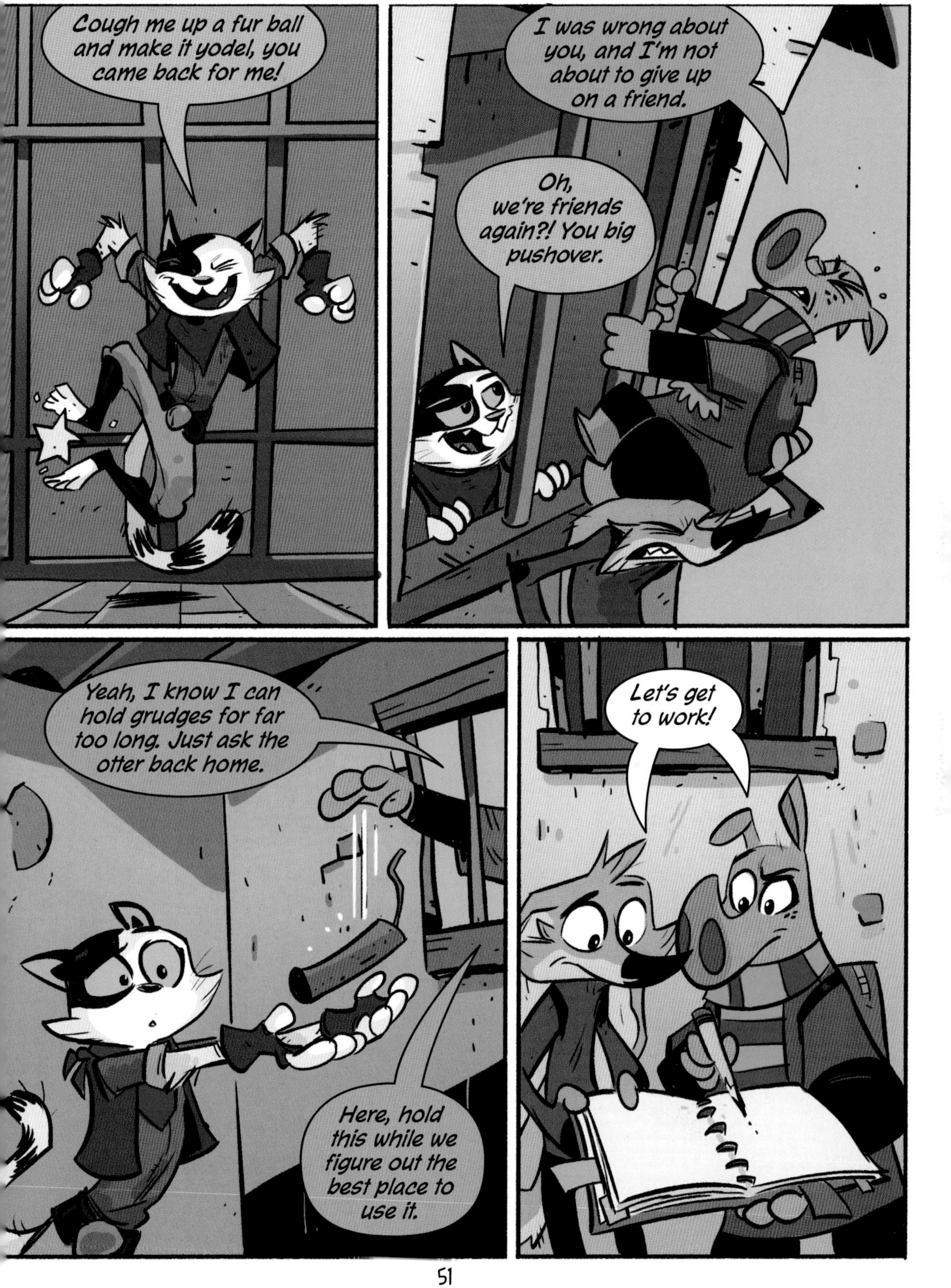
Cough me up a fur ball and make it yodel, you came back for me!
I was wrong about you, and I'm not about to give up on a friend.
Oh, we're friends again?! You big pushover.
Yeah, I know I can hold grudges for far too long. Just ask the otter back home.
Here, hold this while we figure out the best place to use it.
Let's get to work!

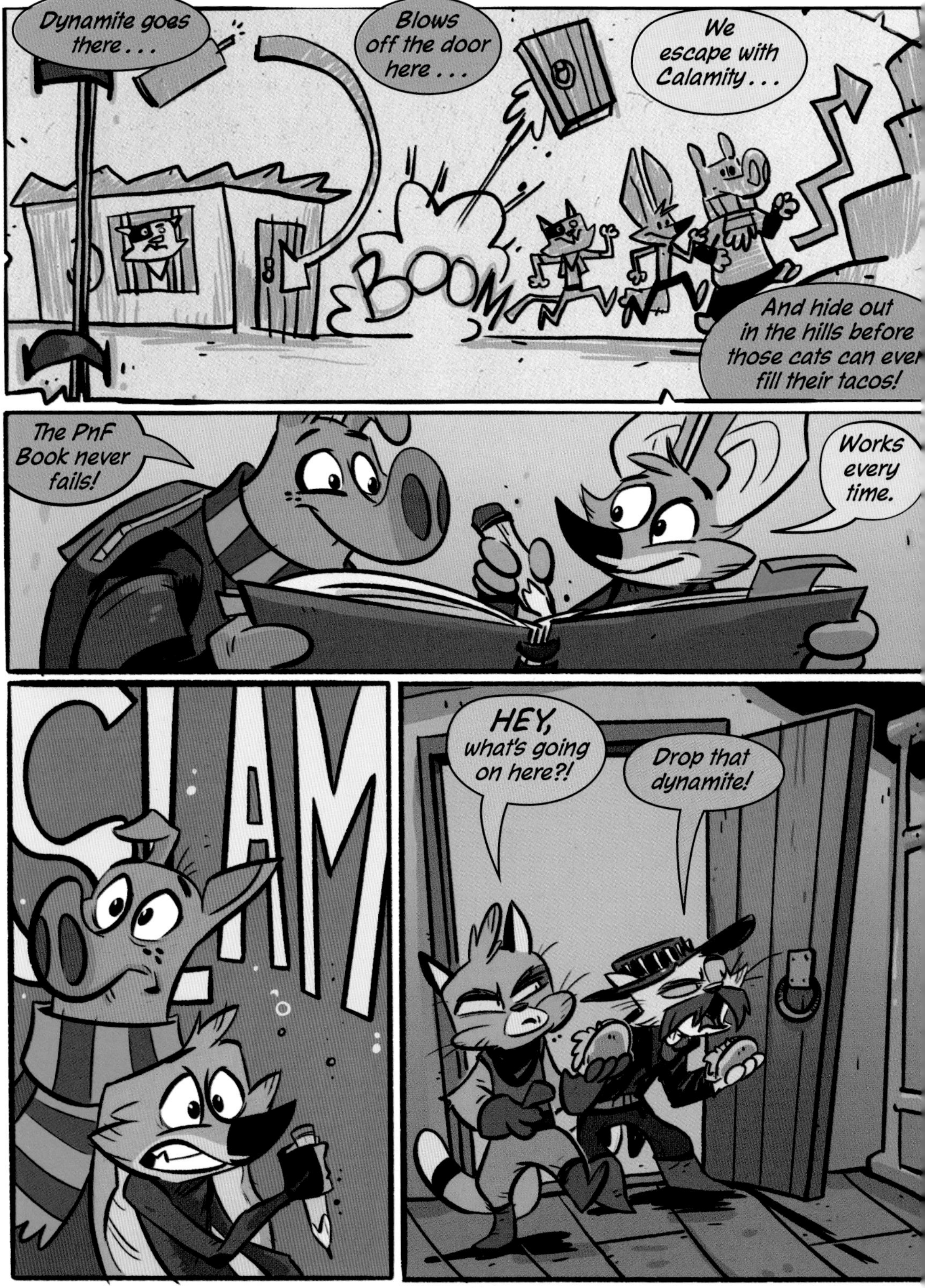
Dynamite goes there . . .
Blows off the door here . . .
We escape with Calamity . . .
BOOM
And hide out in the hills before those cats can ever fill their tacos!
The PnF Book never fails!
Works every time.
CLAM
HEY, what's going on here?!
Drop that dynamite!

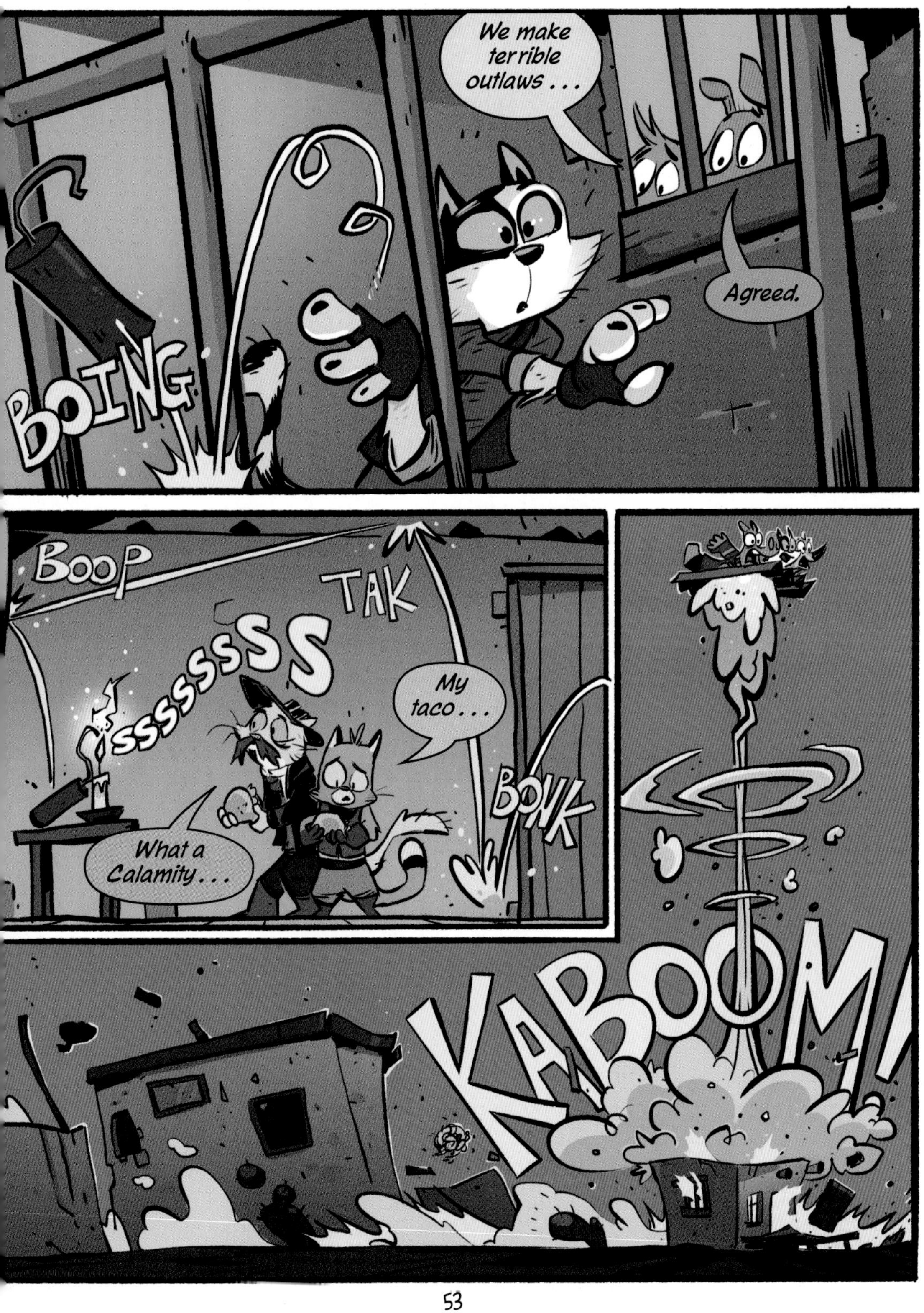
We make terrible outlaws . . .
Agreed.
BOING
BOOP
TAK
SSSSSSSSS
My taco . . .
What a Calamity . . .
BONK
KABOOM!

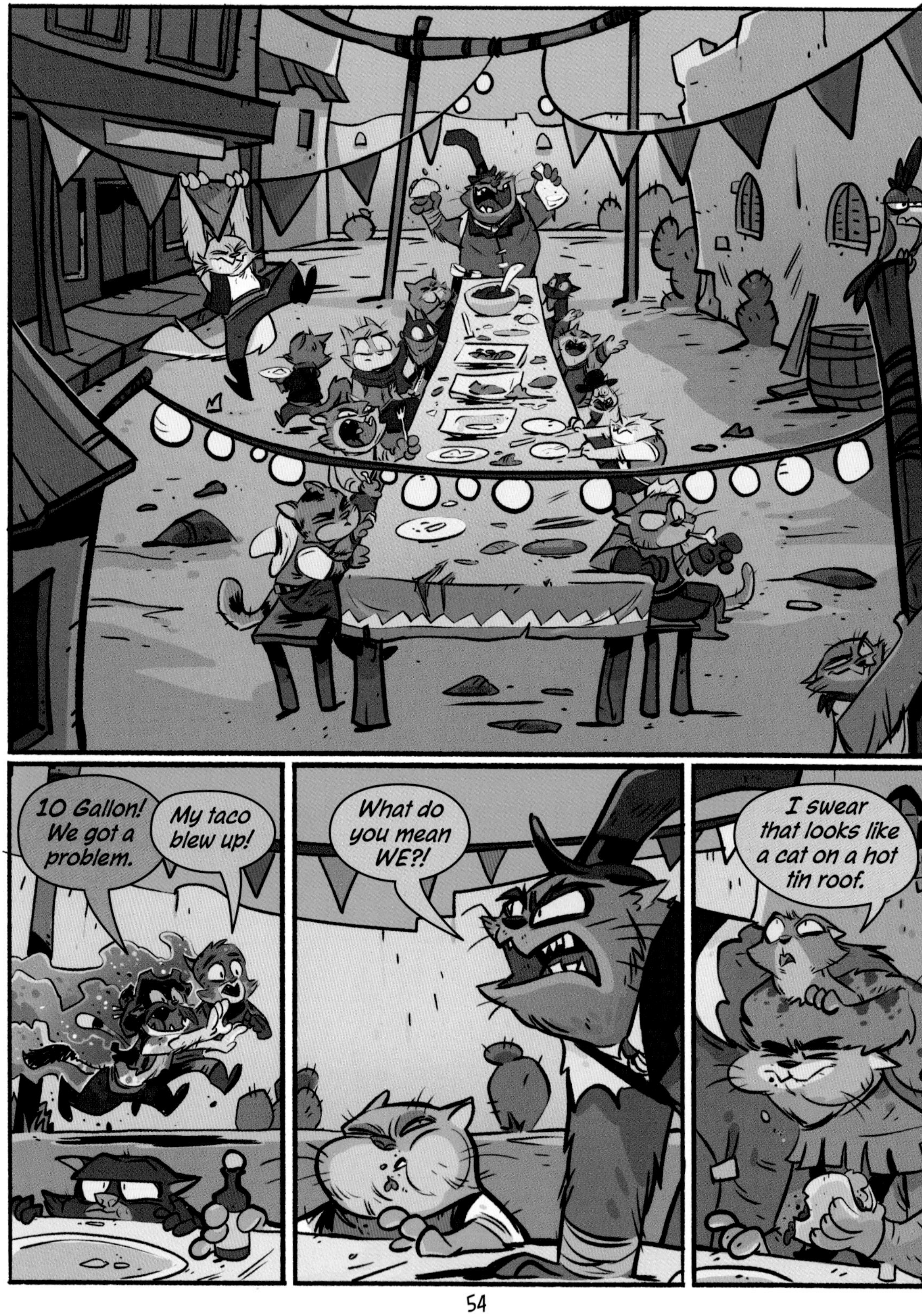
10 Gallon! We got a problem.
My taco blew up!
What do you mean WE?!
I swear that looks like a cat on a hot tin roof.

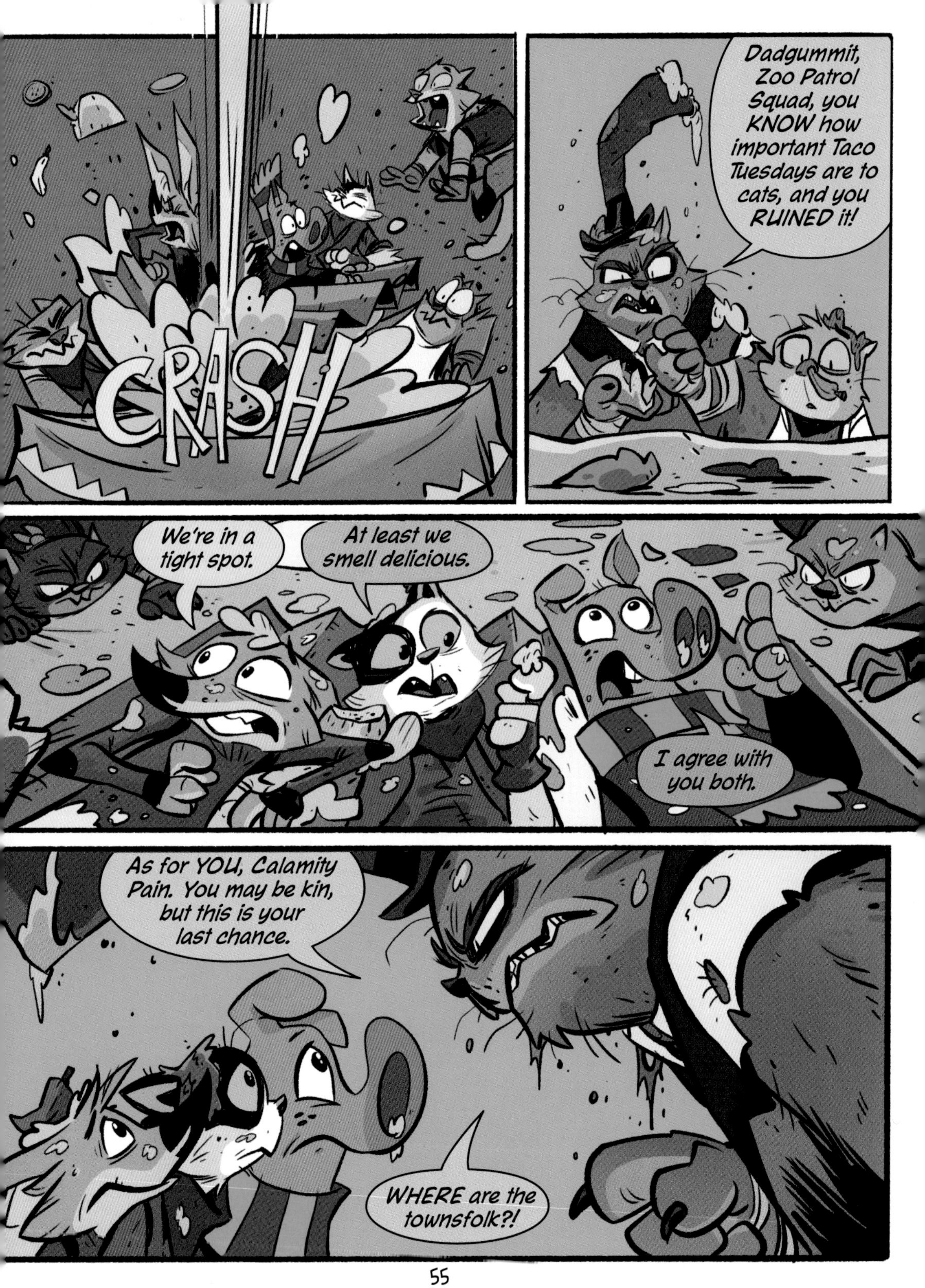
CRASH
Dadgummit, Zoo Patrol Squad, you KNOW how important Taco Tuesdays are to cats, and you RUINED it!
We're in a tight spot.
At least we smell delicious.
I agree with you both.
As for YOU, Calamity Pain. You may be kin, but this is your last chance.
WHERE are the townsfolk?!

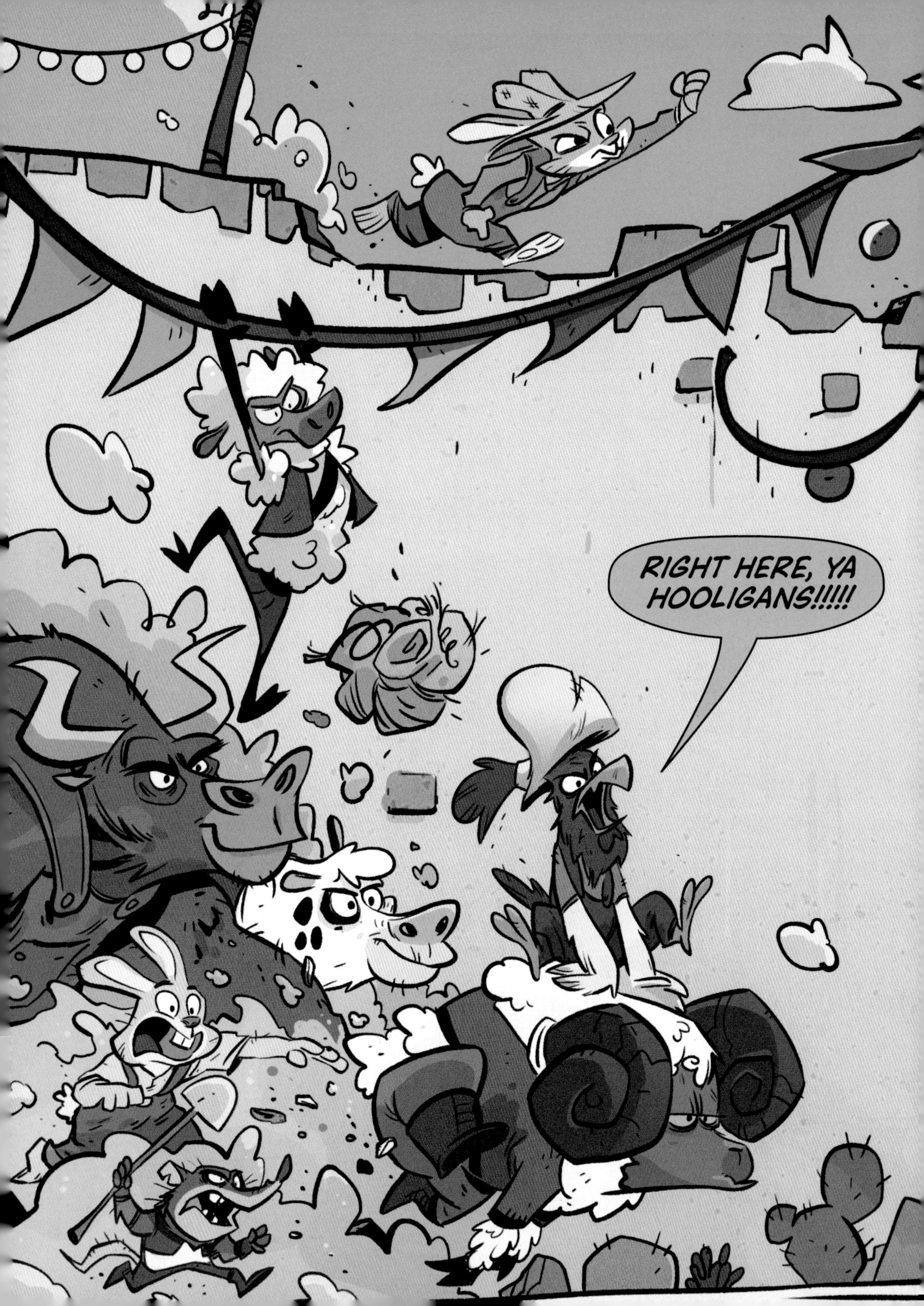
RIGHT HERE, YA HOOLIGANS!!!!!

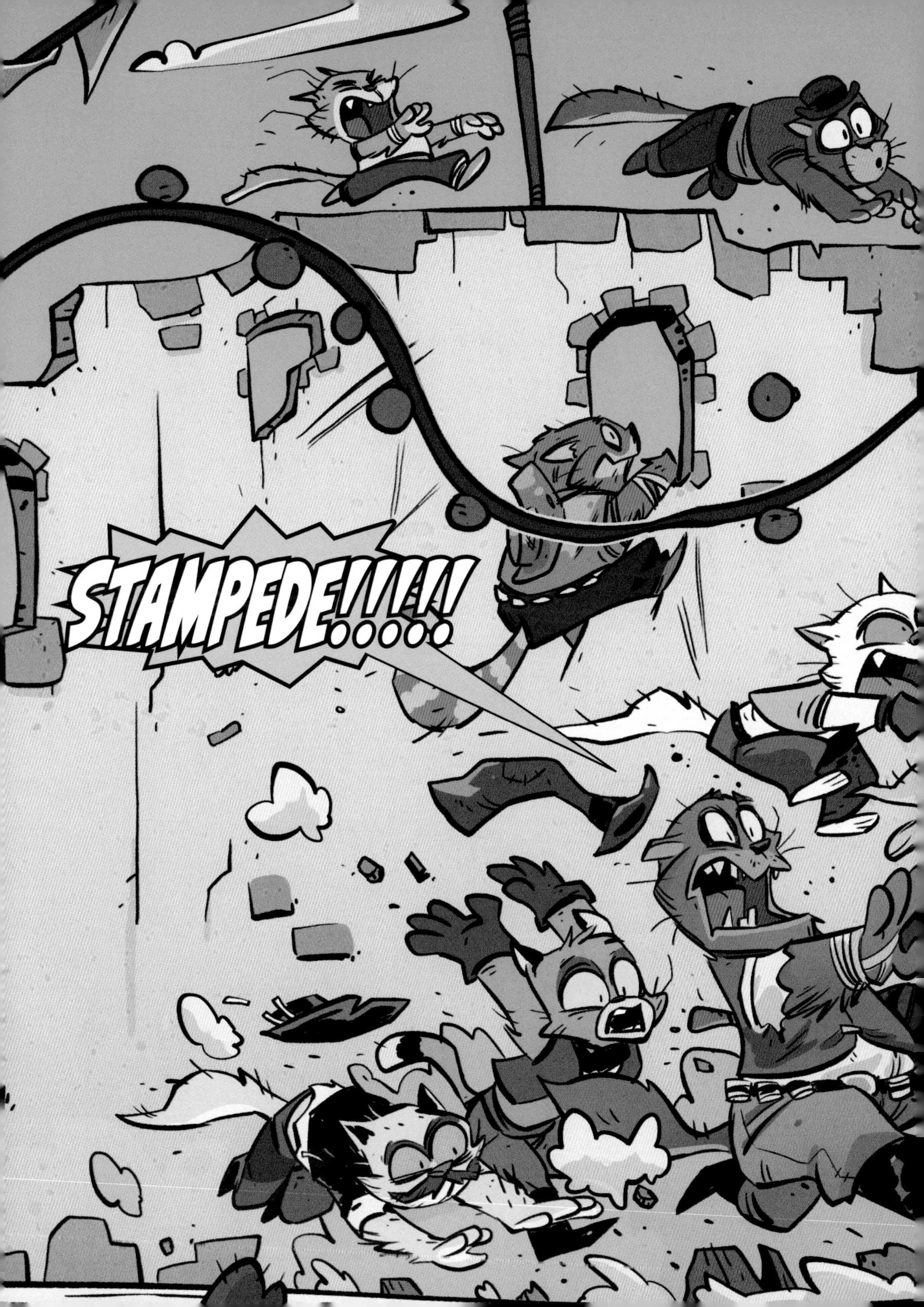
STAMPEDE!!!!!!

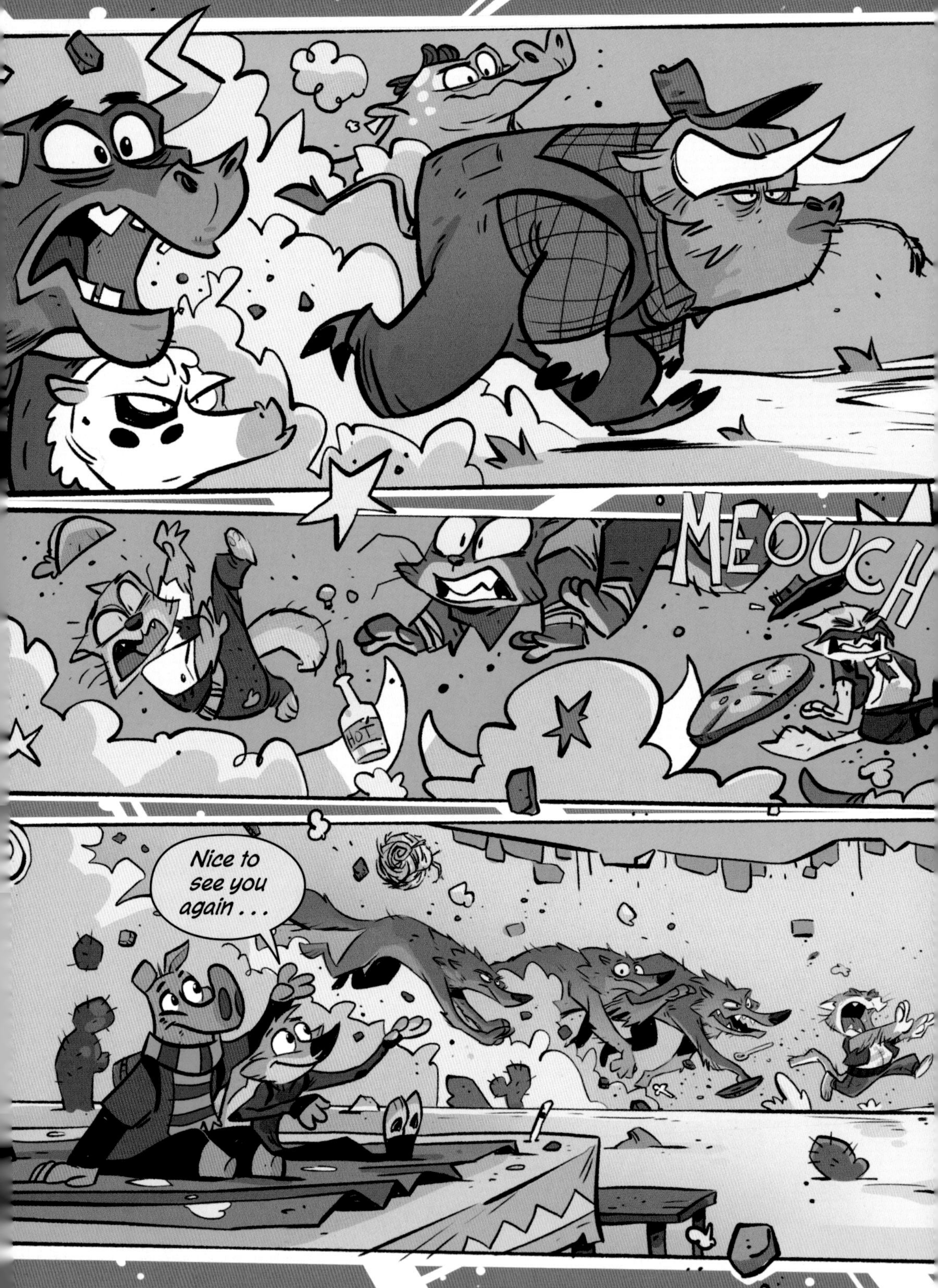
MEOUCH
HOT
Nice to see you again . . .

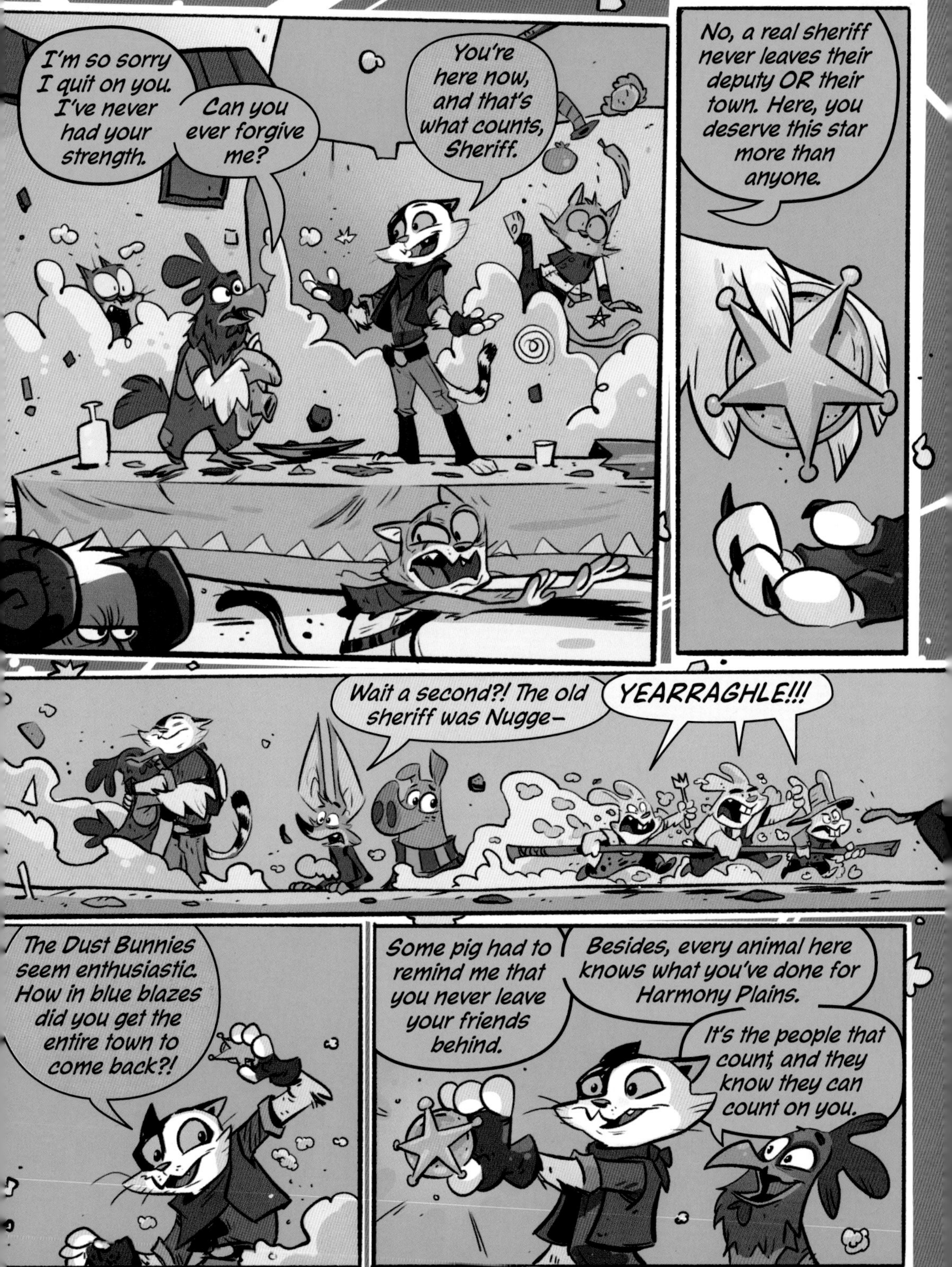

I'm so sorry I quit on you. I've never had your strength.
Can you ever forgive me?
You're here now, and that's what counts, Sheriff.
No, a real sheriff never leaves their deputy OR their town. Here, you deserve this star more than anyone.
Wait a second?! The old sheriff was Nugge—
YEARRAGHLE!!!
The Dust Bunnies seem enthusiastic. How in blue blazes did you get the entire town to come back?!
Some pig had to remind me that you never leave your friends behind.
Besides, every animal here knows what you've done for Harmony Plains.
It's the people that count, and they know they can count on you.

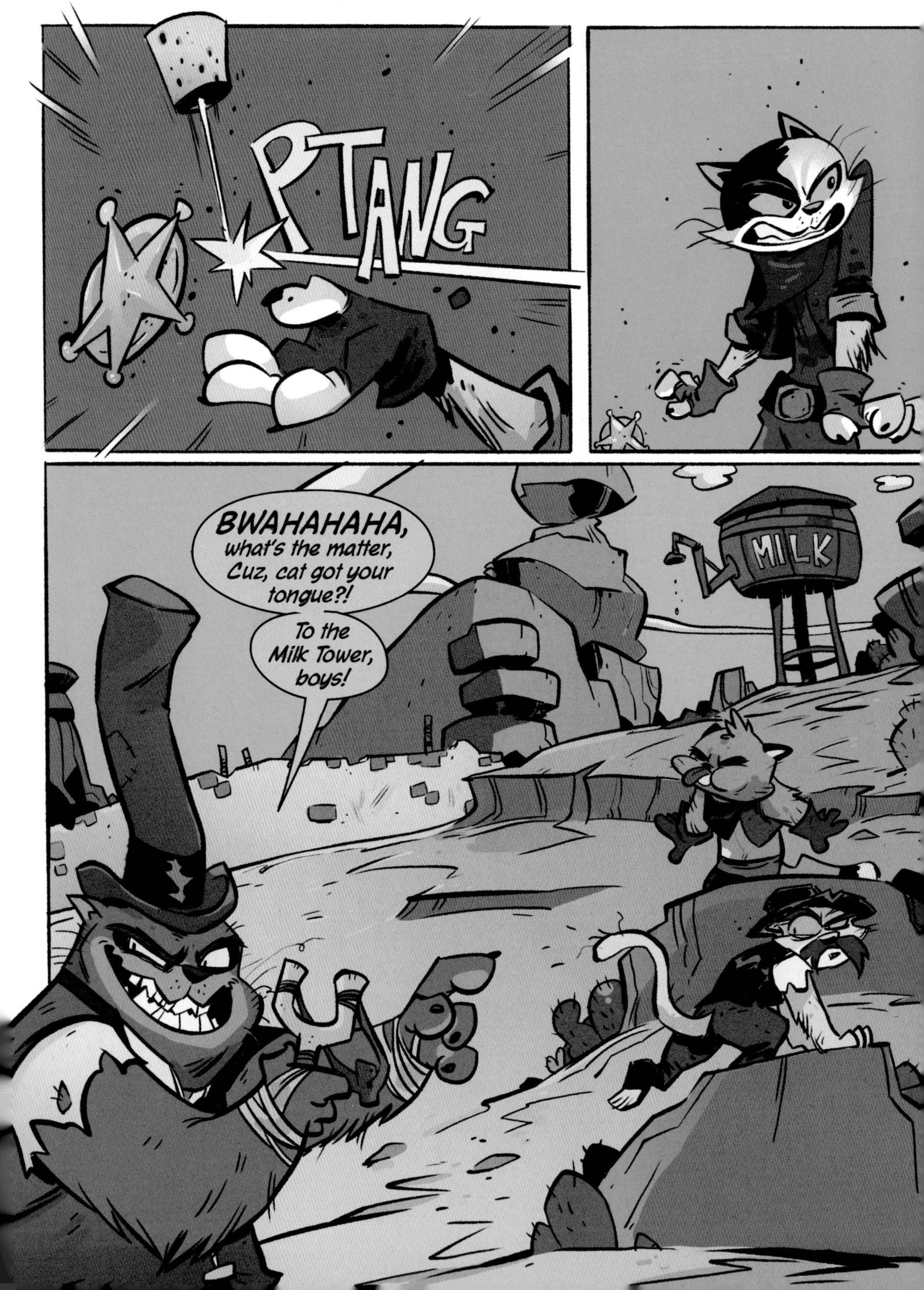
PTANG
BWAHAHAHA, what's the matter, Cuz, cat got your tongue?!
To the Milk Tower, boys!
MILK

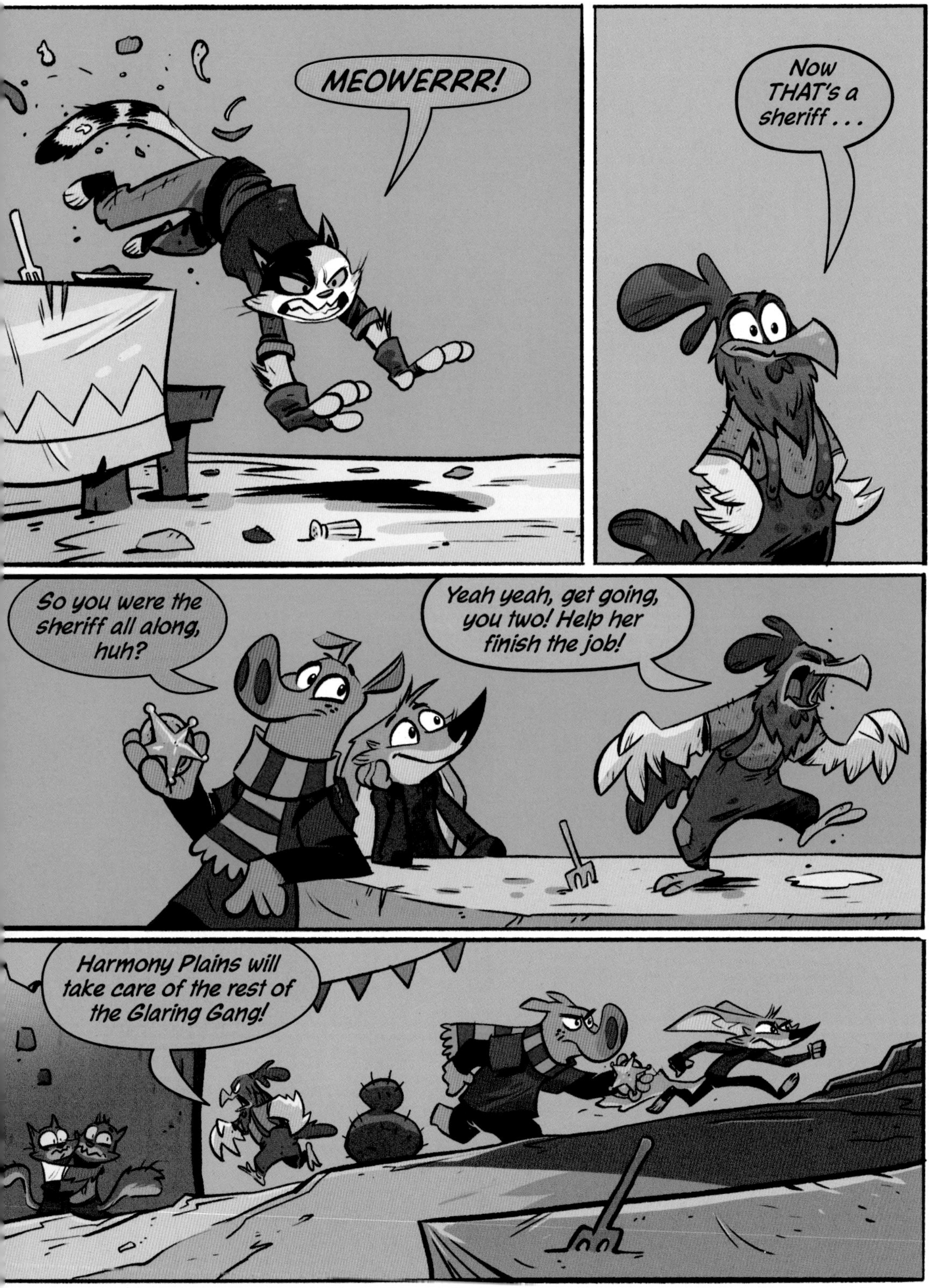
MEOWERRR!
Now THAT's a sheriff . . .
So you were the sheriff all along, huh?
Yeah yeah, get going, you two! Help her finish the job!
Harmony Plains will take care of the rest of the Glaring Gang!

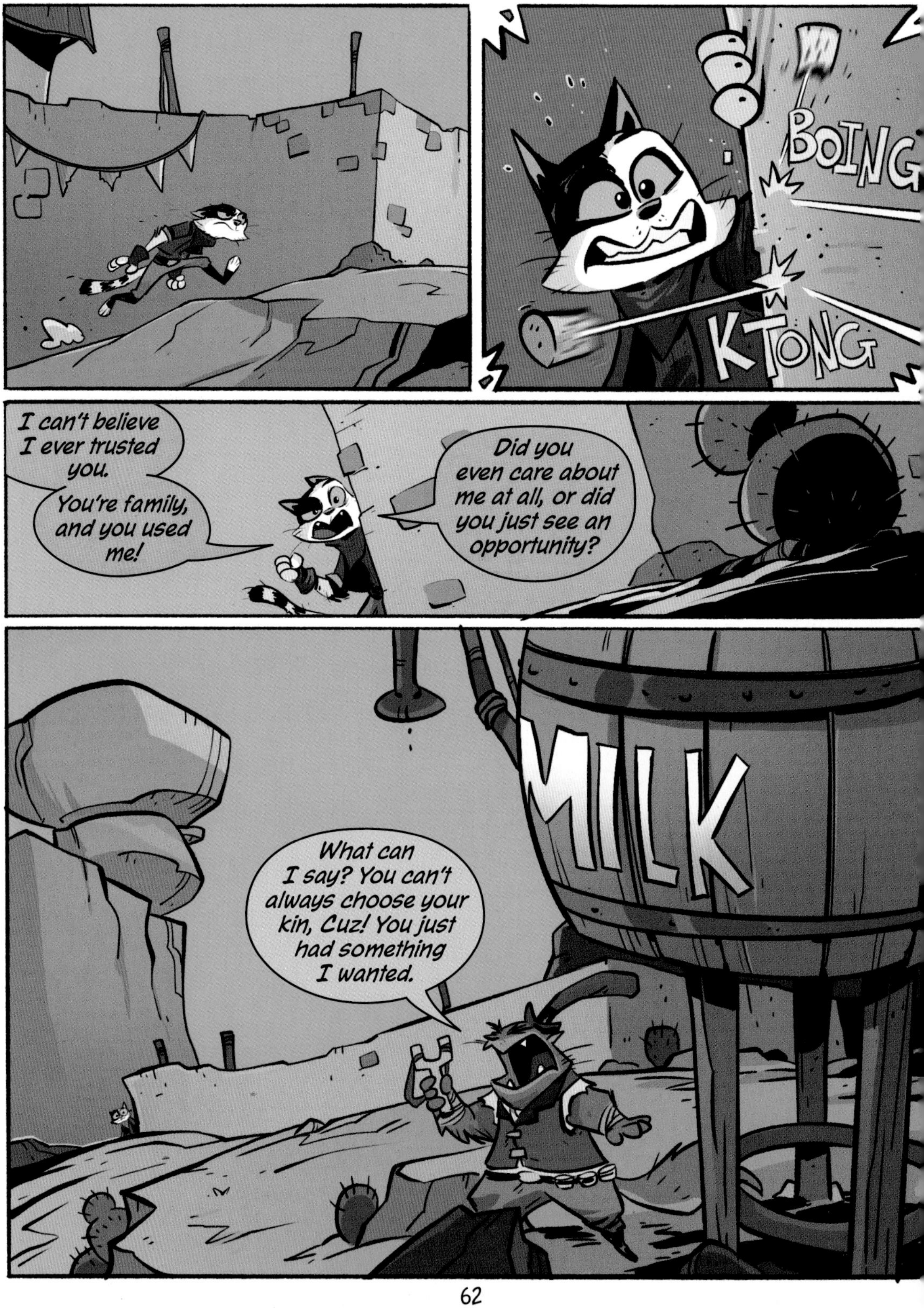
BOING
KTONG
I can't believe I ever trusted you.
You're family, and you used me!
Did you even care about me at all, or did you just see an opportunity?
MILK
What can I say? You can't always choose your kin, Cuz! You just had something I wanted.

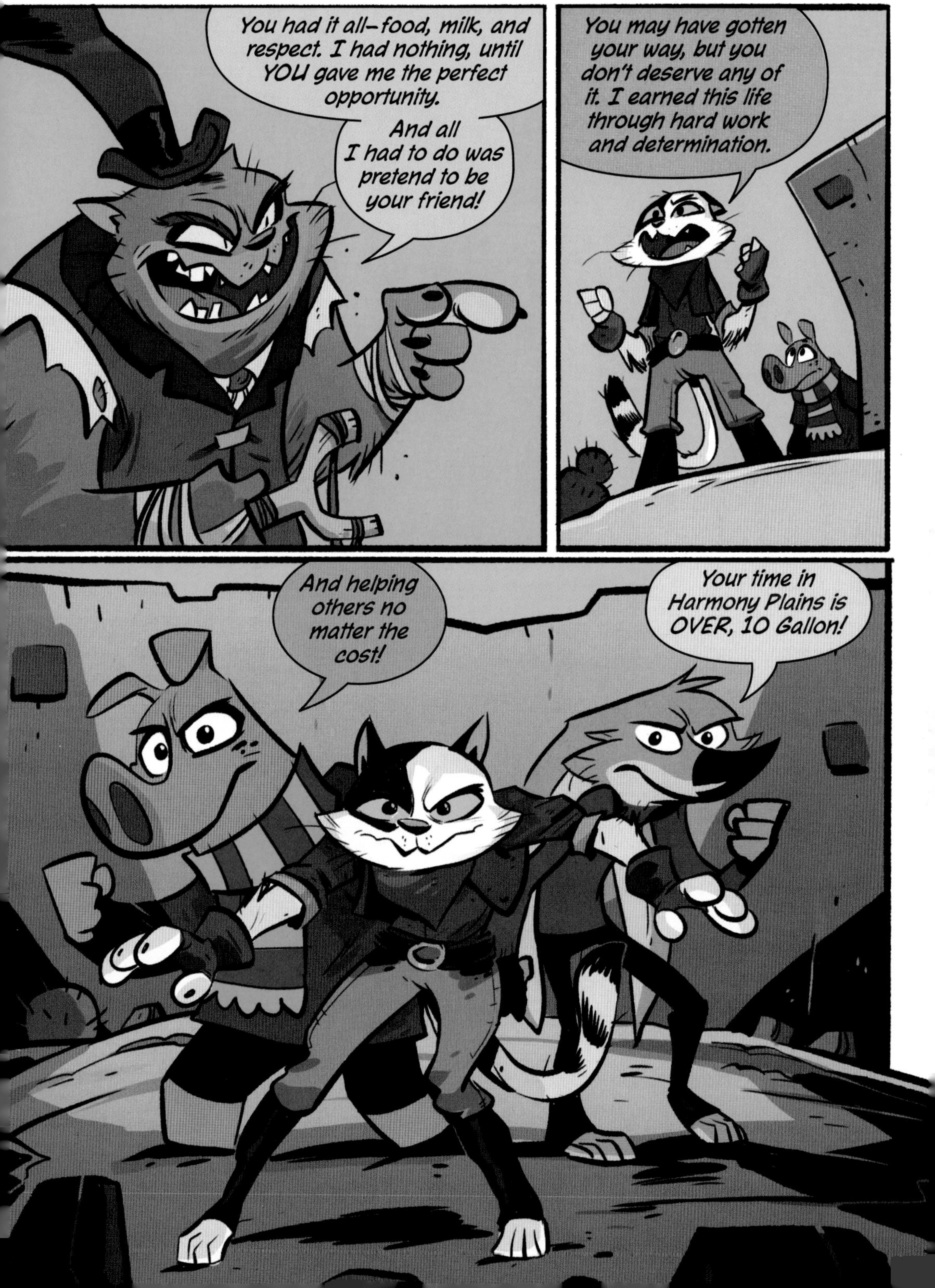
You had it all—food, milk, and respect. I had nothing, until YOU gave me the perfect opportunity.
And all I had to do was pretend to be your friend!
You may have gotten your way, but you don't deserve any of it. I earned this life through hard work and determination.
And helping others no matter the cost!
Your time in Harmony Plains is OVER, 10 Gallon!

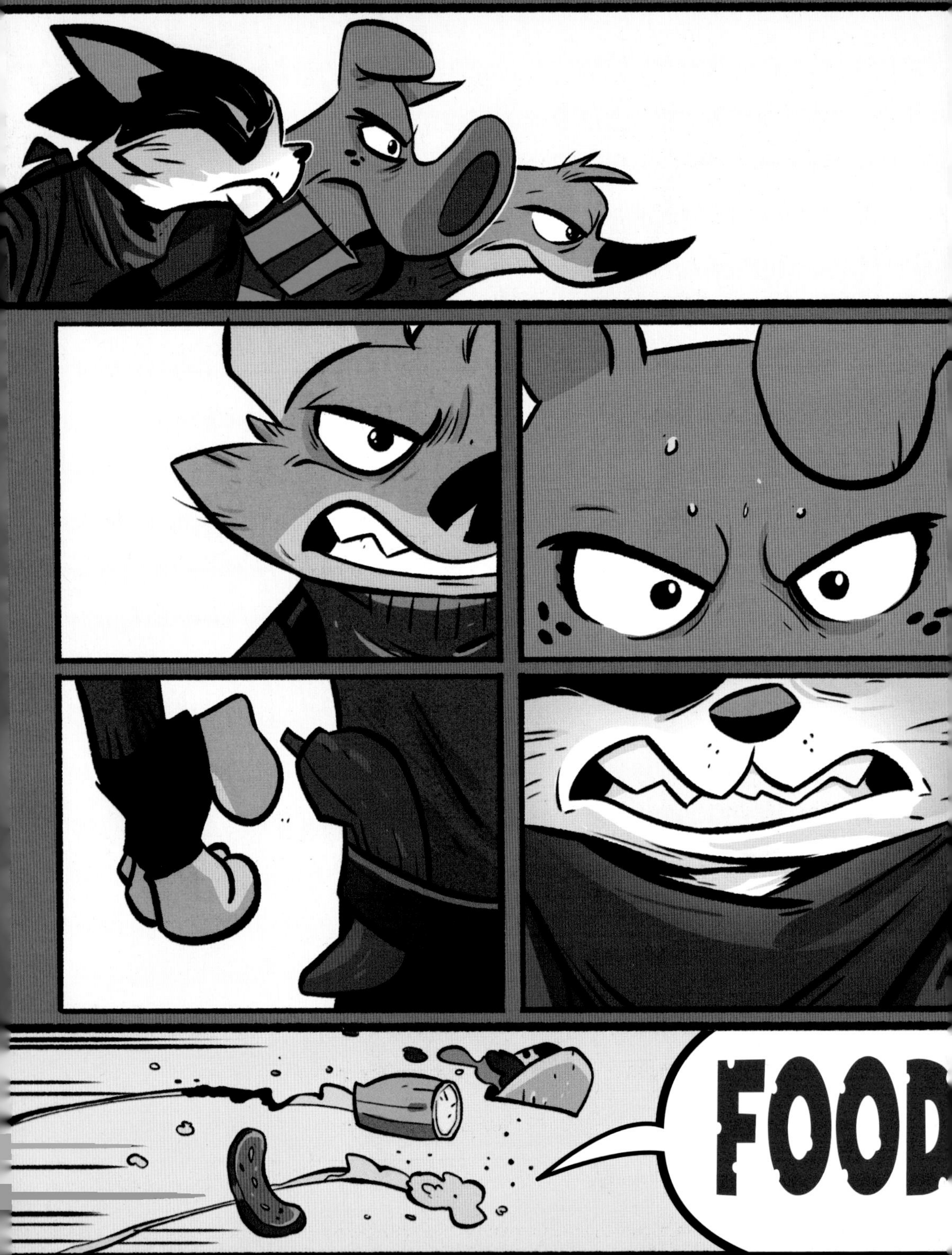
FOOD

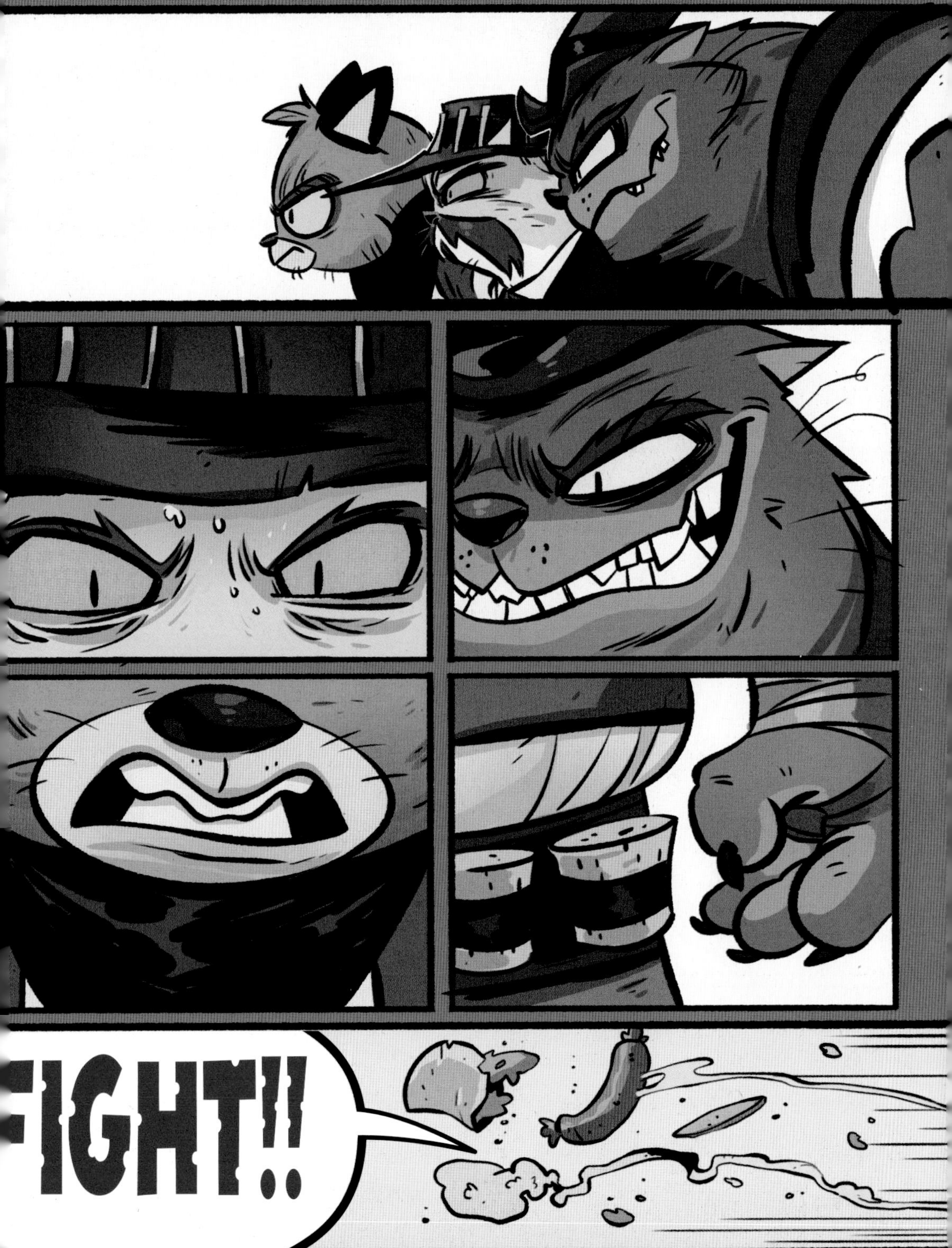
FIGHT!!

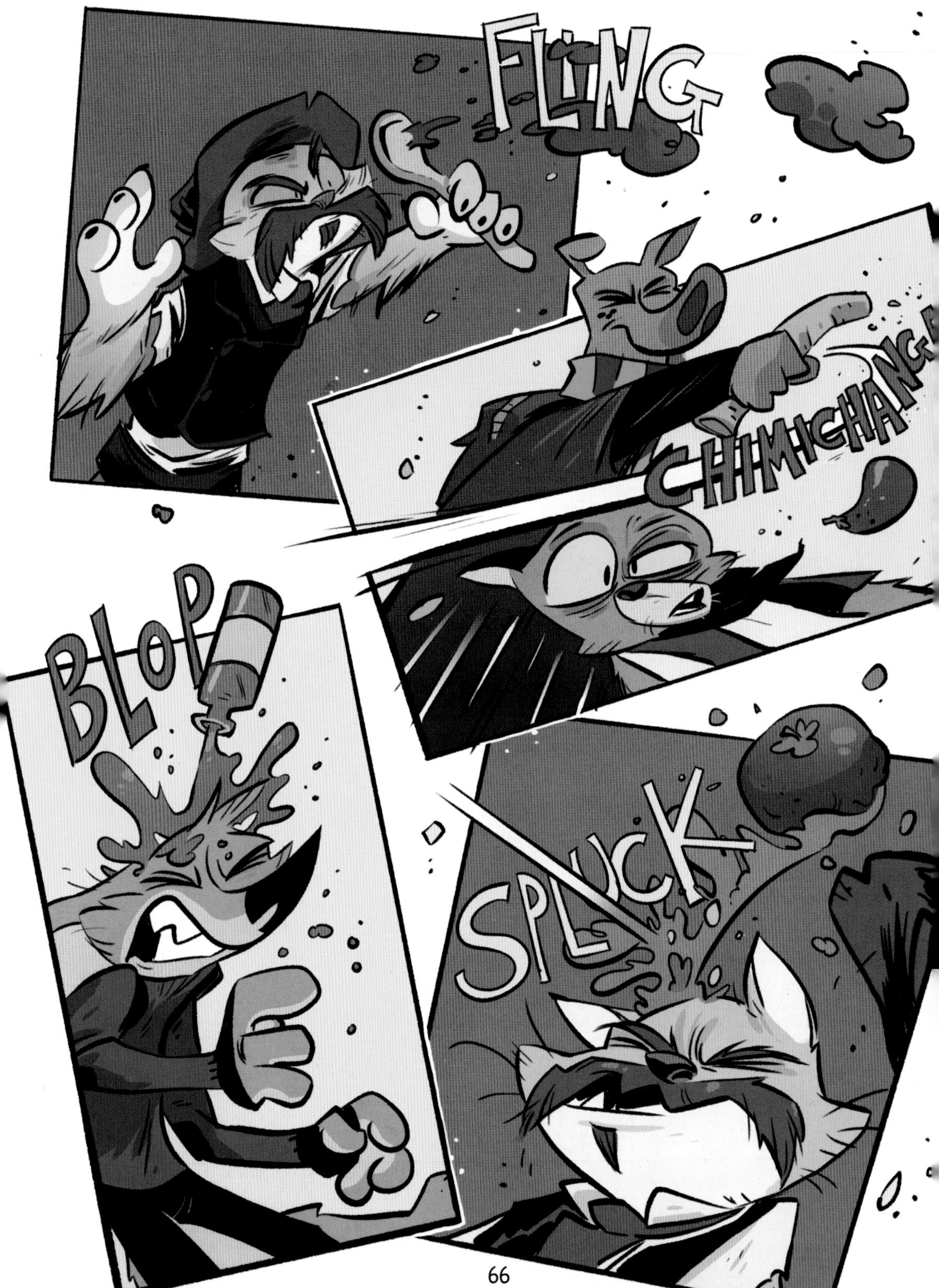
FLING
CHIMICHANGA
BLOP
SPLUCK

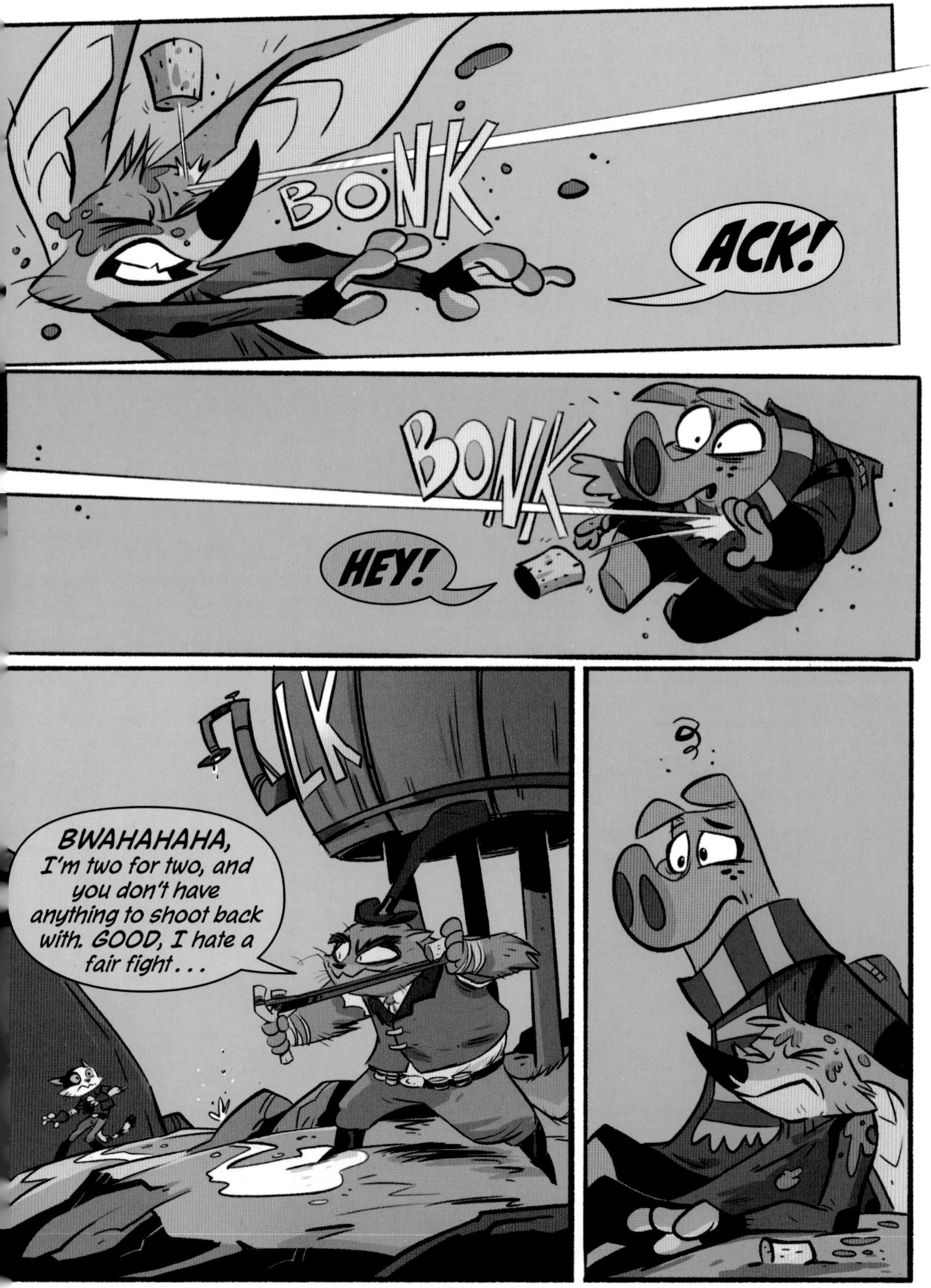
BONK
ACK!
BONK
HEY!
BWAHAHAHA, I'm two for two, and you don't have anything to shoot back with. GOOD, I hate a fair fight...

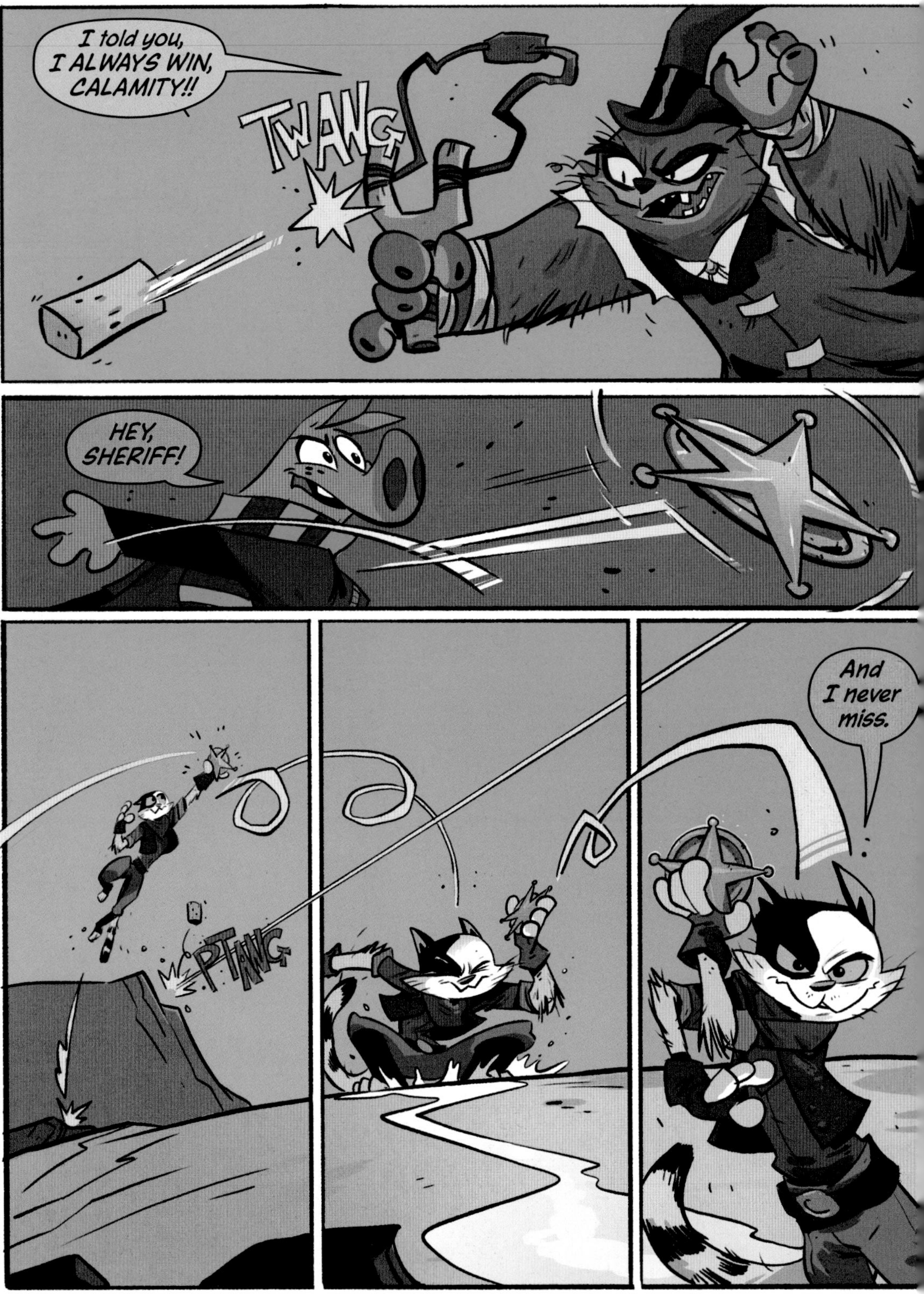
I told you, I ALWAYS WIN, CALAMITY!!
TWANG
HEY, SHERIFF!
PTANG
And I never miss.

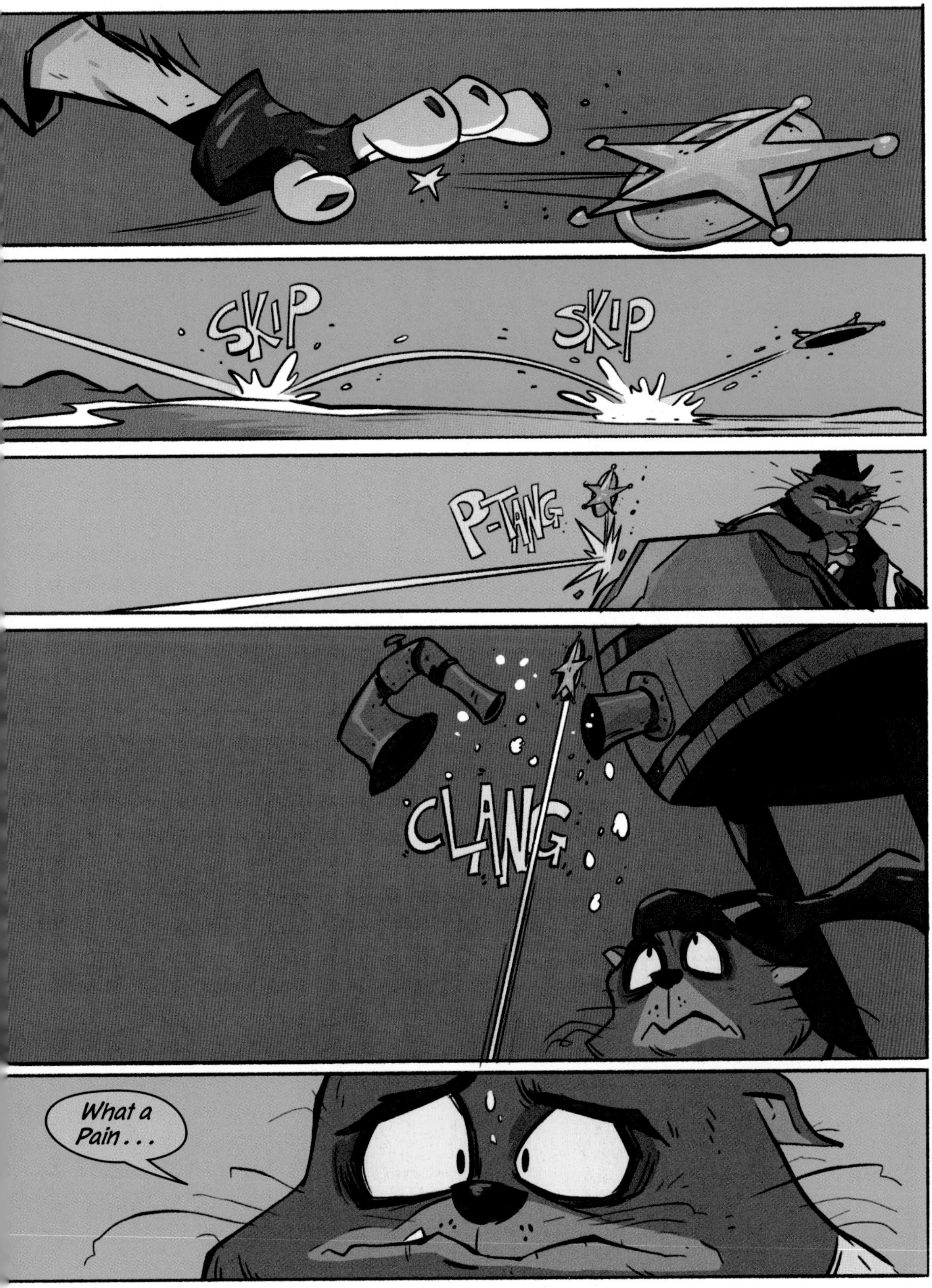
SKIP
SKIP
P-TANG
CLANG
What a Pain...

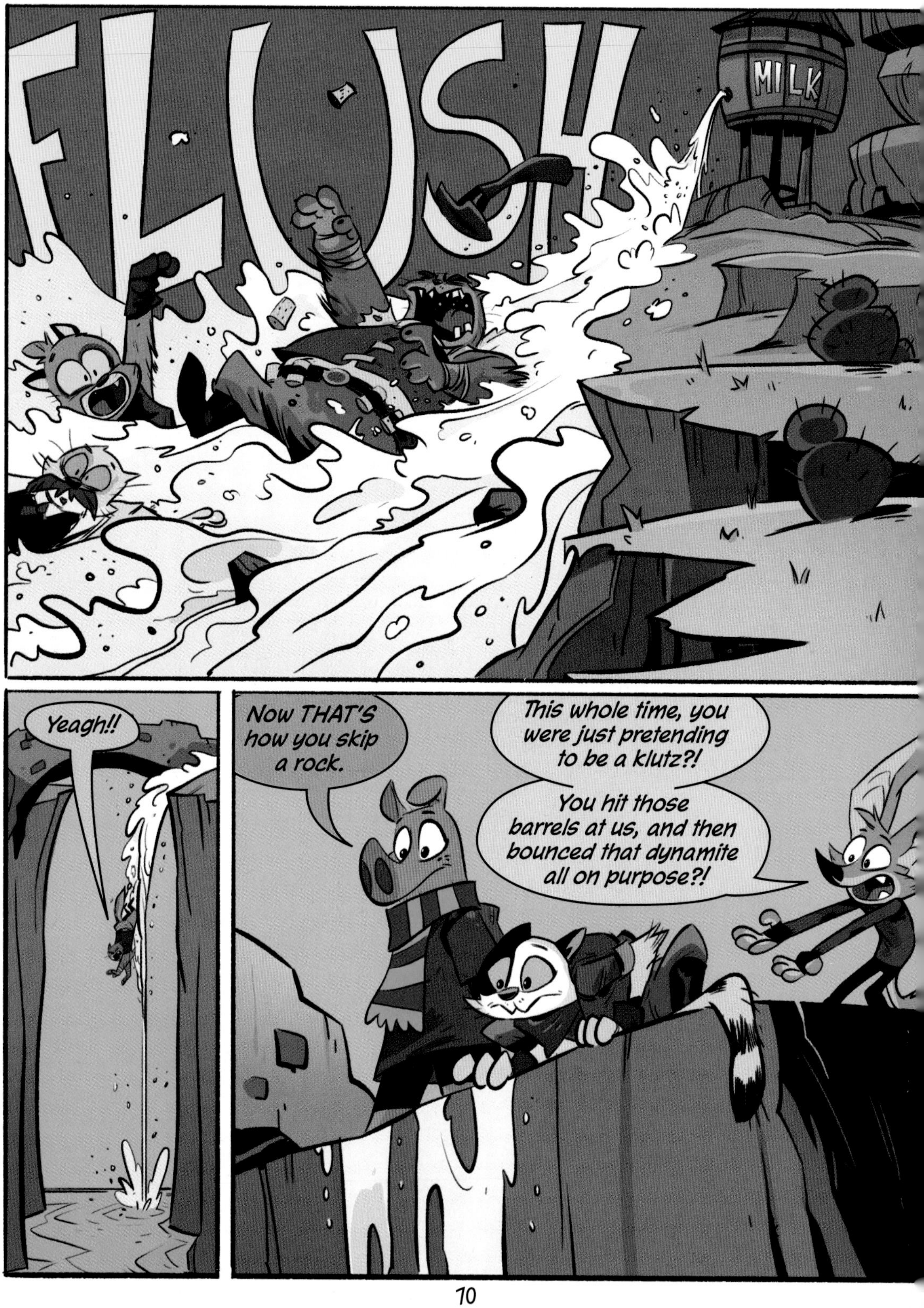
FLUSH
MILK
Yeagh!!
Now THAT'S how you skip a rock.
This whole time, you were just pretending to be a klutz?!
You hit those barrels at us, and then bounced that dynamite all on purpose?!

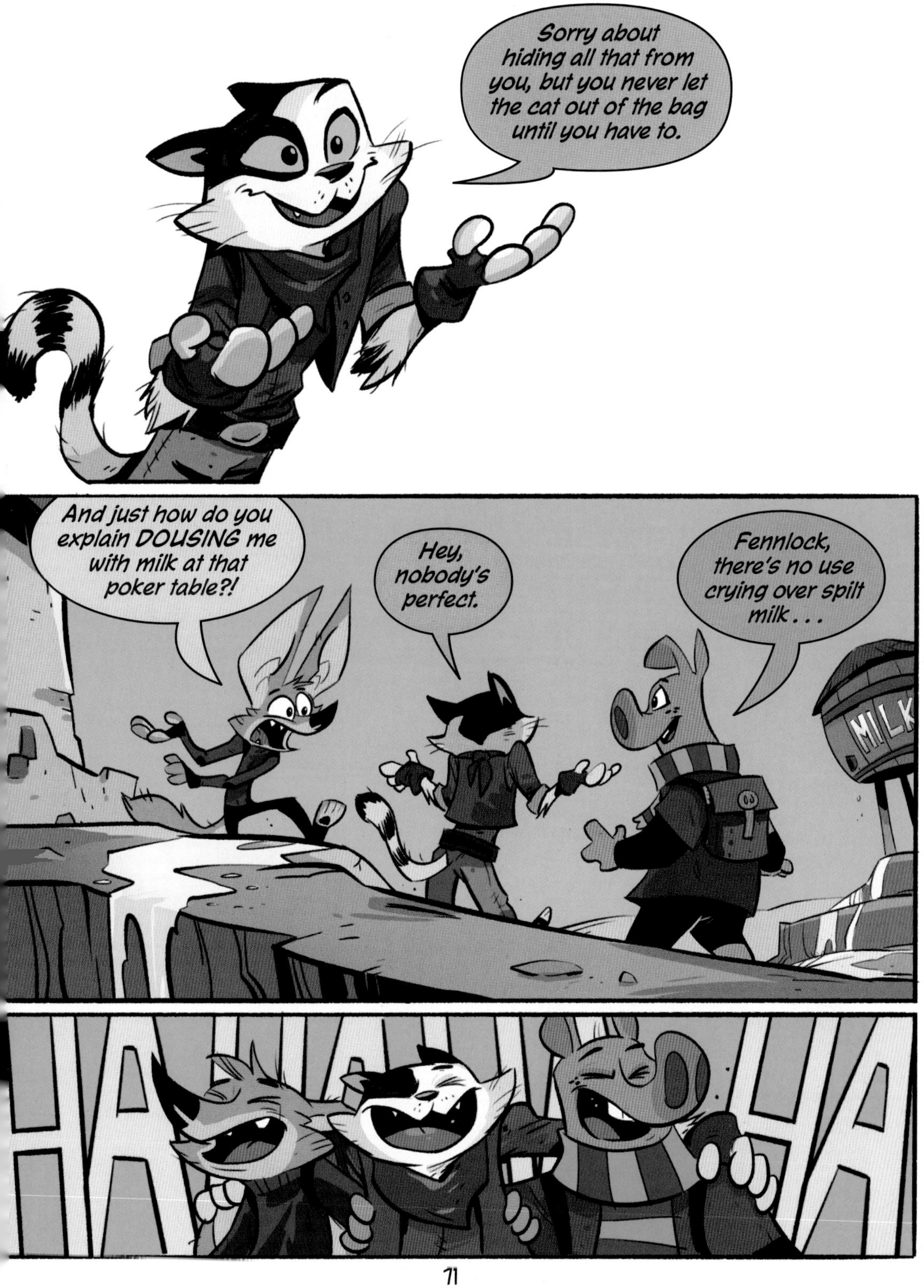
Sorry about hiding all that from you, but you never let the cat out of the bag until you have to.
And just how do you explain DOUSING me with milk at that poker table?!
Hey, nobody's perfect.
Fennlock, there's no use crying over spilt milk . . .
MILK

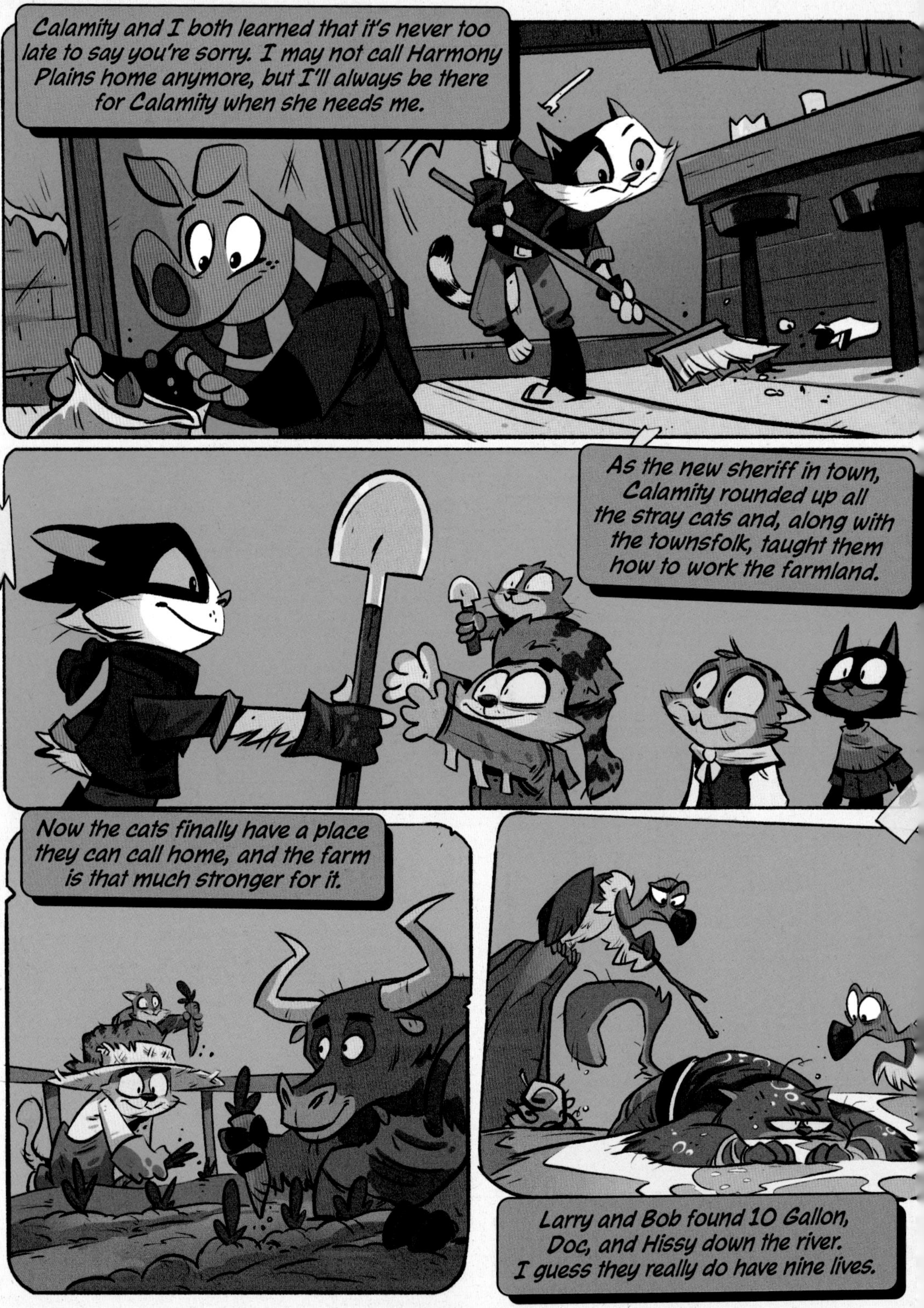
Calamity and I both learned that it's never too late to say you're sorry. I may not call Harmony Plains home anymore, but I'll always be there for Calamity when she needs me.
As the new sheriff in town, Calamity rounded up all the stray cats and, along with the townsfolk, taught them how to work the farmland.
Now the cats finally have a place they can call home, and the farm is that much stronger for it.
Larry and Bob found 10 Gallon, Doc, and Hissy down the river. I guess they really do have nine lives.

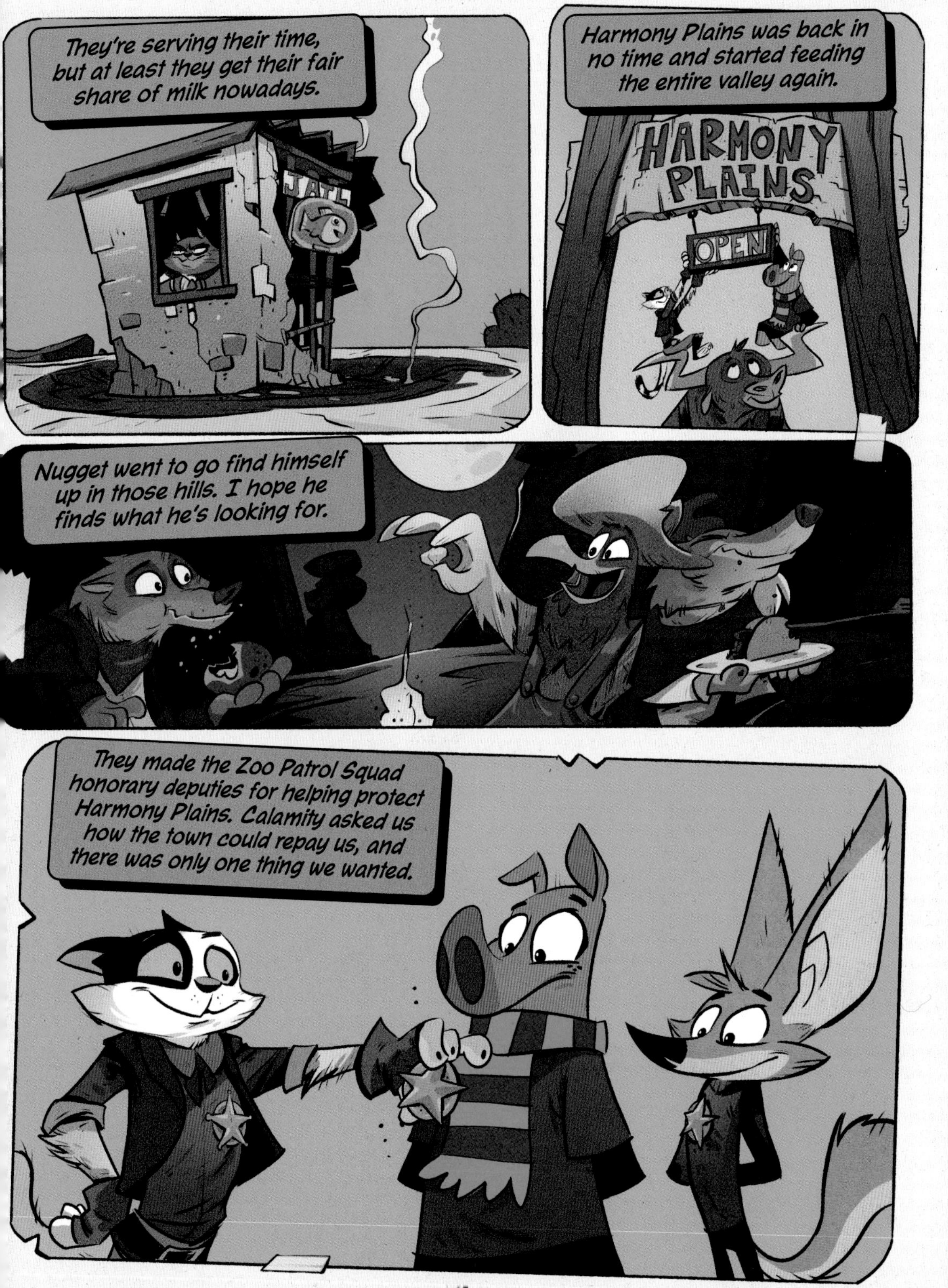
They're serving their time, but at least they get their fair share of milk nowadays.
JAIL
Harmony Plains was back in no time and started feeding the entire valley again.
HARMONY PLAINS
OPEN
Nugget went to go find himself up in those hills. I hope he finds what he's looking for.
They made the Zoo Patrol Squad honorary deputies for helping protect Harmony Plains. Calamity asked us how the town could repay us, and there was only one thing we wanted.

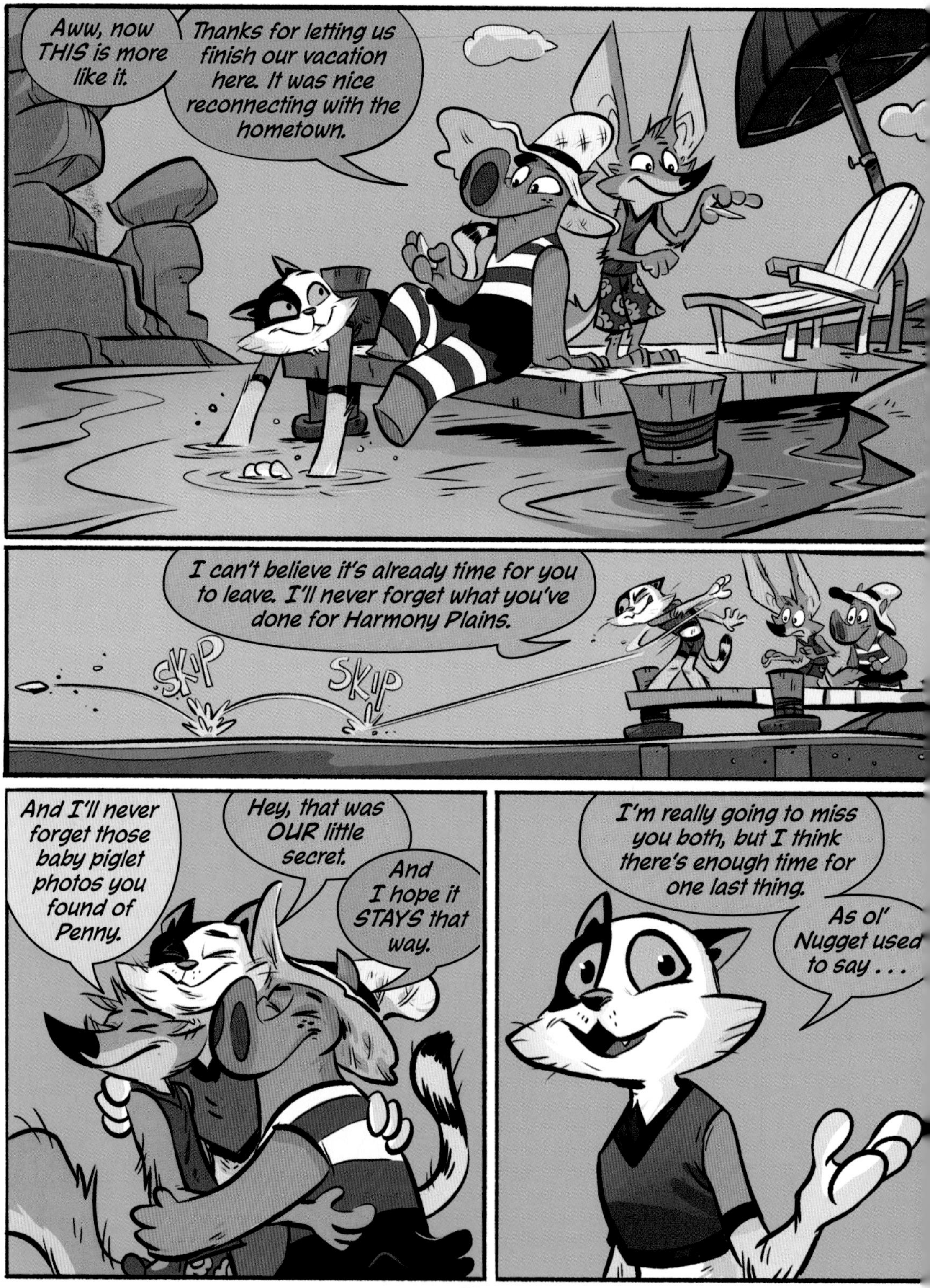
Aww, now THIS is more like it.
Thanks for letting us finish our vacation here. It was nice reconnecting with the hometown.
I can't believe it's already time for you to leave. I'll never forget what you've done for Harmony Plains.
SKIP
SKIP
And I'll never forget those baby piglet photos you found of Penny.
Hey, that was OUR little secret.
And I hope it STAYS that way.
I'm really going to miss you both, but I think there's enough time for one last thing.
As ol' Nugget used to say . . .

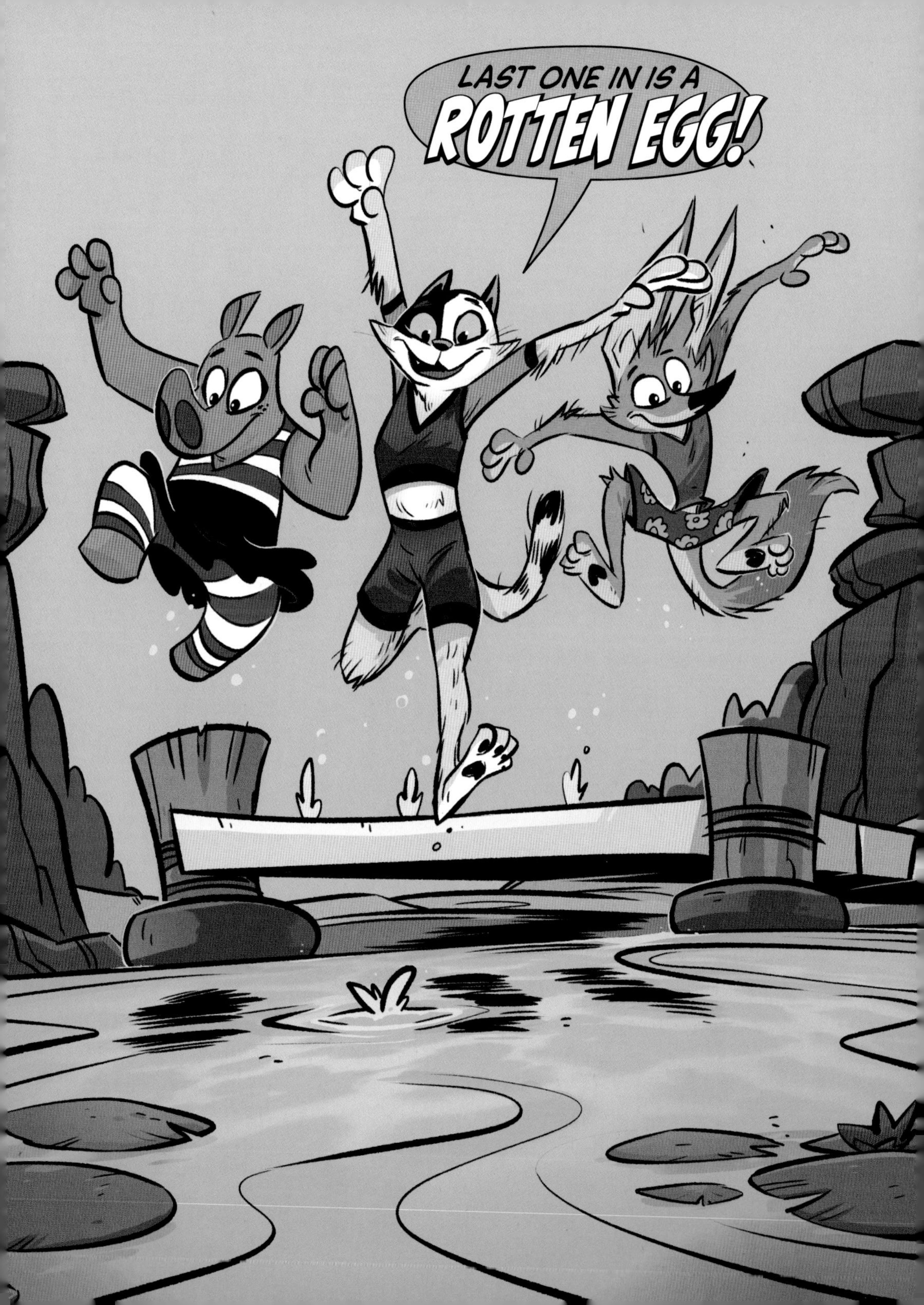
LAST ONE IN IS A ROTTEN EGG!

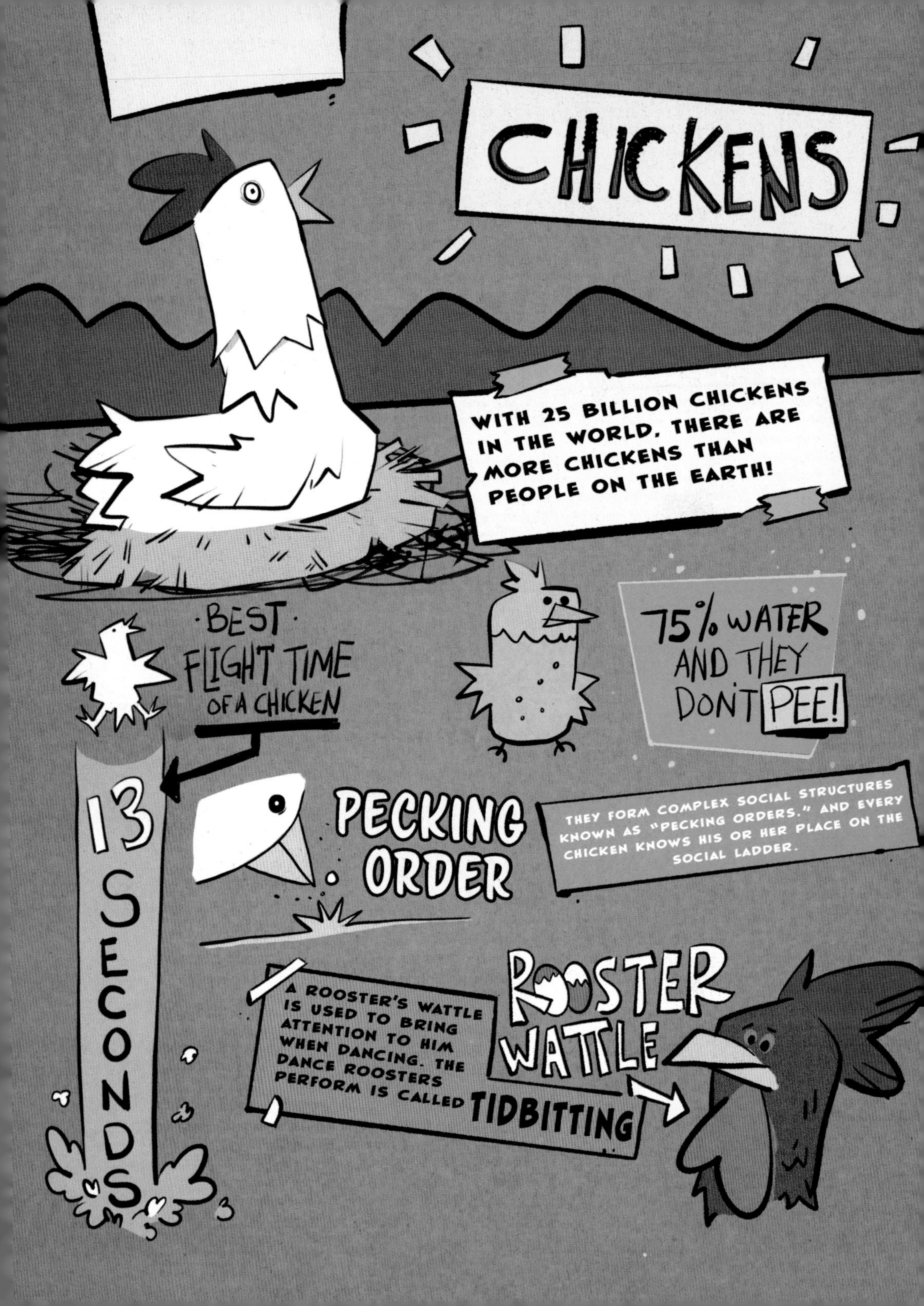
CHICKENS
WITH 25 BILLION CHICKENS IN THE WORLD, THERE ARE MORE CHICKENS THAN PEOPLE ON THE EARTH!
·BEST· FLIGHT TIME OF A CHICKEN
13 SECONDS
75% WATER AND THEY DON'T PEE!
PECKING ORDER
THEY FORM COMPLEX SOCIAL STRUCTURES KNOWN AS "PECKING ORDERS," AND EVERY CHICKEN KNOWS HIS OR HER PLACE ON THE SOCIAL LADDER.
ROOSTER WATTLE
A ROOSTER'S WATTLE IS USED TO BRING ATTENTION TO HIM WHEN DANCING. THE DANCE ROOSTERS PERFORM IS CALLED TIDBITTING

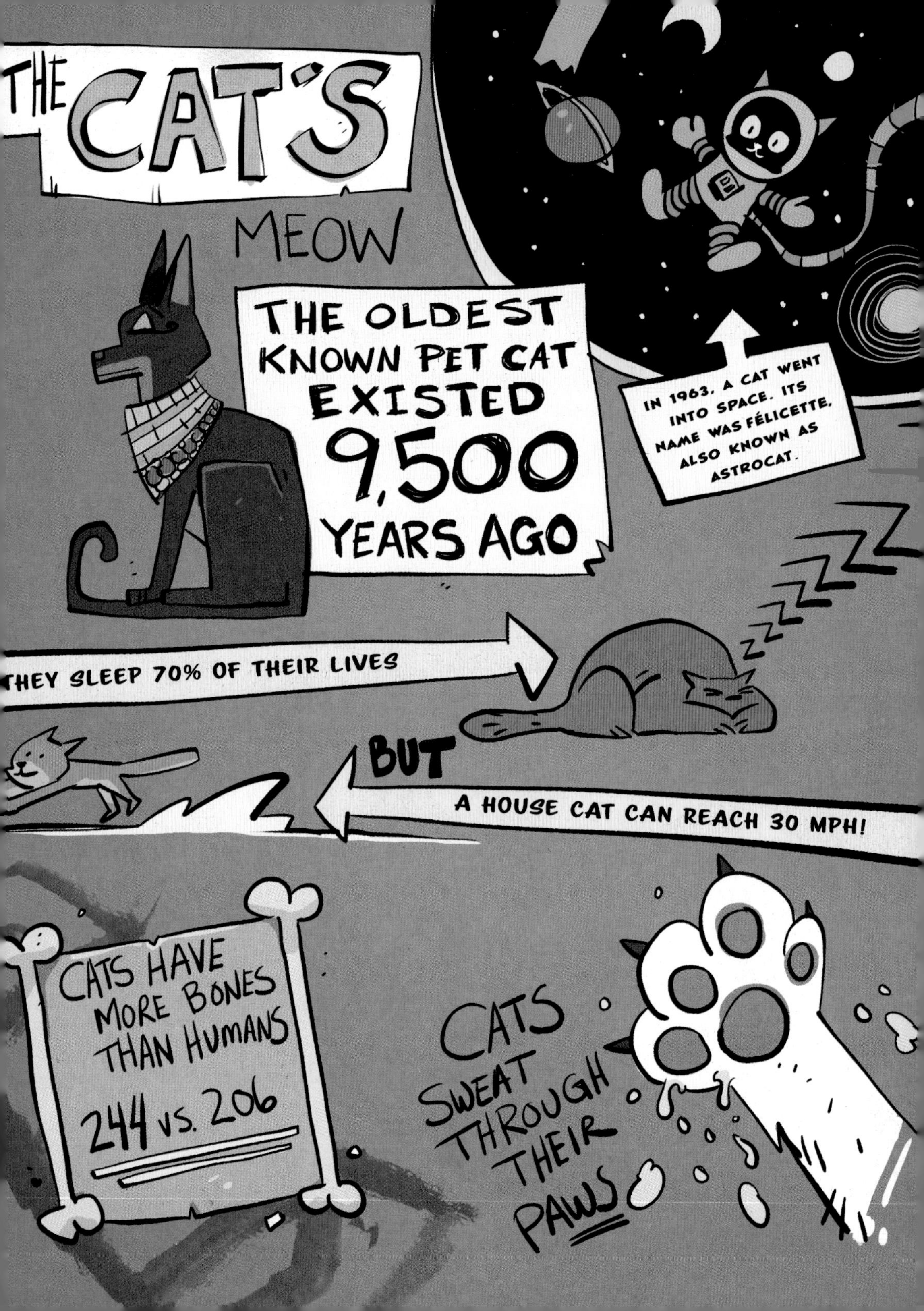

THE CAT'S MEOW
THE OLDEST KNOWN PET CAT EXISTED 9,500 YEARS AGO
IN 1963, A CAT WENT INTO SPACE. ITS NAME WAS FÉLICETTE, ALSO KNOWN AS ASTROCAT.
THEY SLEEP 70% OF THEIR LIVES
ZZZZZZ
BUT
A HOUSE CAT CAN REACH 30 MPH!
CATS HAVE MORE BONES THAN HUMANS
244 VS. 206
CATS SWEAT THROUGH THEIR PAWS

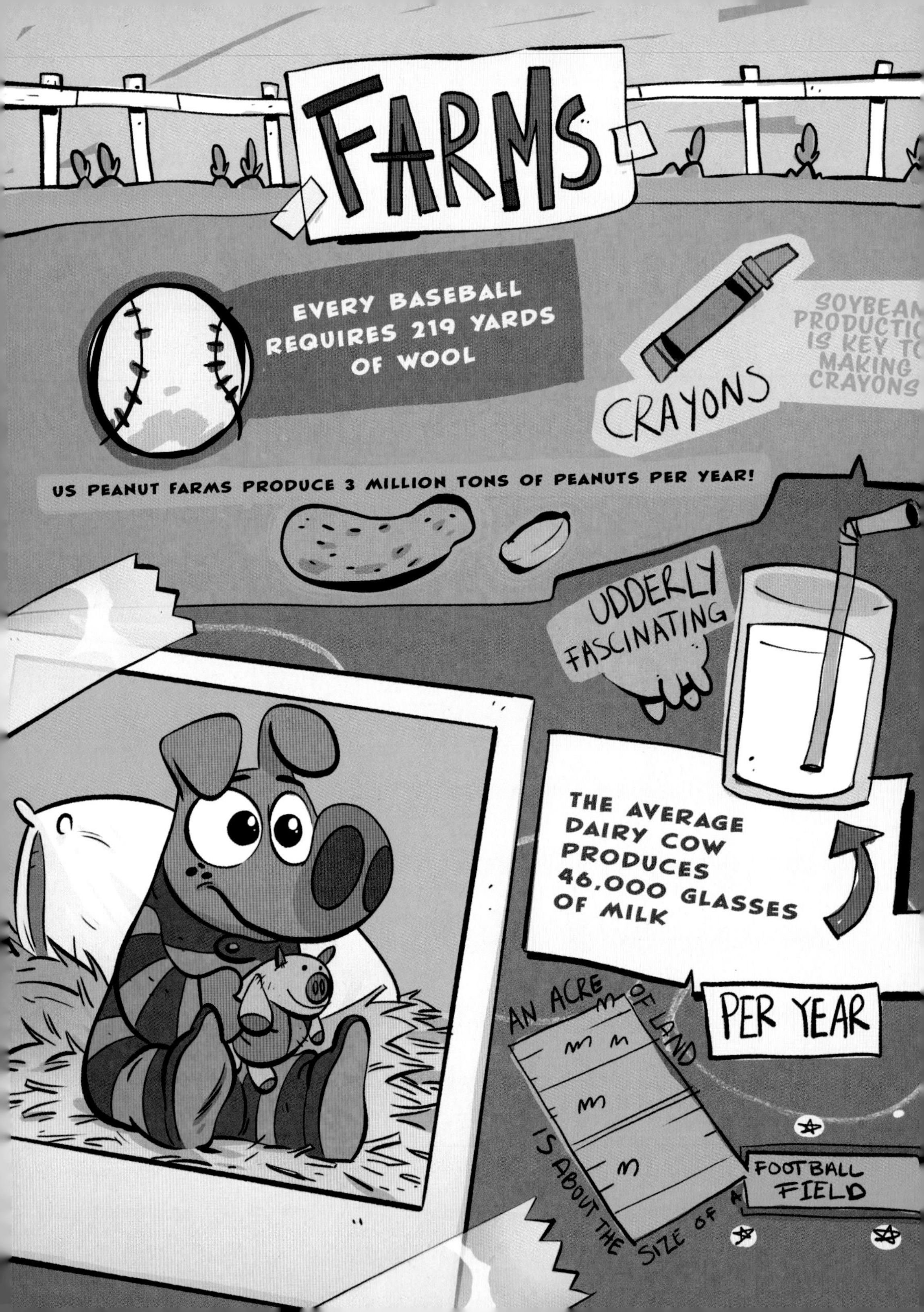
FARMS
EVERY BASEBALL REQUIRES 219 YARDS OF WOOL
CRAYONS
SOYBEAN PRODUCTIO IS KEY TO MAKING CRAYONS
US PEANUT FARMS PRODUCE 3 MILLION TONS OF PEANUTS PER YEAR!
UDDERLY FASCINATING
THE AVERAGE DAIRY COW PRODUCES 46,000 GLASSES OF MILK
PER YEAR
AN ACRE OF LAND IS ABOUT THE SIZE OF A FOOTBALL FIELD